A CORK IN A STORM

A Hippies Search for Truth

VINCENT LAWLER

A Cork in a Storm
Copyright © 2025 by Vincent Lawler

All rights reserved. No part of this publication may be reproduced, distributed, or transmitted in any form or by any means, including photocopying, recording, or other electronic or mechanical methods, without the prior written permission of the author, except in the case of brief quotations embodied in critical reviews and certain other non-commercial uses permitted by copyright law.

tellwell

Tellwell Talent
www.tellwell.ca

ISBN
978-1-77962-899-2 (Paperback)

Table of Contents

Foreword v
Glossary of Terms vii
Chapter 1:   Indonesia 1
Chapter 2:   Malaysia 13
Chapter 3:   Thailand 27
Chapter 4:   India 36
Chapter 5:   Nepal 43
Chapter 6:   Middle East 55
Chapter 7:   Europe 63
Chapter 8:   England 73
Chapter 9:   Wales 80
Chapter 10: Ireland 94
Chapter 11: Scotland 103
Chapter 12: London 114

Foreword

Courage comes in many forms, but courage to accept the truth, to believe in the truth and identify the truth comes to people with no prejudice.

In 1973, the world was crying out for peace. A group of hippies thrown together in Kathmandu debated many topics in search of the truth. God, religion and the creation of the universe were all covered in a quest for the meaning of life, a question asked by each generation that comes along. It is a broad question with many avenues to explore, yet after thousands of years the question is still asked. Curiosity has shaped our world through the ages and curiosity arrives with each generation searching for answers. These fun, truth-seeking hippies formed the People's World Council and convened with a naivety, born out of a thirst for knowledge.

Mibald Zytchalot enjoyed being part of the council that would visit many countries and cultures in this quest for a long sought-after answer. That mystery would not be the only mystery that the unfortunately named Mibald Zytchalot would encounter. The Hippie Trail was an adventurist trek overland to India, travelling from the east or west in the early seventies, and "My Balls Itch a Lot" had set off from Darwin on a ten-thousand-mile overland adventure to England. His journey incorporated a spiritual adventure absorbing unfamiliar cultures, whilst all the time being unaware that an intriguing drama was being played out around him. It was not until he reached the UK that he realised how deeply involved he was. Many more miles would get covered as the drama unfolded in a chase through England, Ireland, Scotland and Wales.

He was a cork in a storm.

Glossary of Terms

Richard III: Turd

Jollyferkating: Contented and happy

6RAR: Sixth Royal Australian Regiment

Apotik: Pharmacy (Indonesia)

Becak: Bicycle rickshaw (Malaysia)

R&R: Rest and recreation

Didi Mau: Get Lost (Vietnam)

Uc Dai Loi: Australian (Vietnam)

Goitre: Enlarged thyroid growth on neck

Burma: now Myanmar

Calcutta: now Kolkata

Bidis: cheap leaf smoke (India)

Yugoslavia: now divided into Bosnia and Herzegovina, Croatia, Montenegro, Serbia, North Macedonia, Slovenia and Kosovo

"Keep right on to the end of the road": Scottish song from the 1920s

Crook: Unwell (Australia)

Pie-Floater: Pie in pea soup (Adelaide delicacy)

Qu, Qu, Qu: Go, Go, Go (China)

Bludger: Australian humorous greeting

Oyabun: Triad gang leader

Chapter One

Indonesia

A large *Richard III* was steaming majestically through the water, glistening in the hot midday sun. Its size could not be ignored; it had appeared from behind the end of a jetty with a Hessian modesty screen. Miles had just finished his business and was walking off the jetty when to his horror, some little boys on the bank started trying to sink the *Bismark*, bombarding the embarrassing target with stones from the shore. Miles was mortified as he walked away from the jetty, somewhere in the sweltering heat of Sumatra.

It was early March 1973, when he was travelling on a bus bound for Padang, He had been travelling on buses and locomotives for days, through Java and Sumatra, eating nothing but rice and the occasional hard-boiled egg. The bus had made its regular food stop on this long journey for the passengers to stretch out, eat, and use the amazing toilet facilities. Miles had learned from experience that you would feel full too early by eating slow; he had observed that, by contrast, shovelling in rice with the fingers as fast as you could at these eating places would sustain you till the next stop.

The young boys cheered and laughed at his discomfort, as did the passengers on the bus, who were all friendly people returning home to Padang. Miles was the only Westerner. He was a fit and handsome young man with long, curly blond hair and a red moustache, every bit the image of a hippie traveller. He was loving every moment of every day passing through this tropical and rugged terrain. He was well acclimatised, as only six weeks before, Miles had flown from Darwin, in the top end of Australia, to the wonderful unique island of Bali where he spent a month jollyferkating and exploring the fabulous Balinese culture.

He had been fascinated with Southeast Asia from the moment he landed in Bali. It felt like a different world and he instantly wanted to stay. He had spent twelve months in Vietnam a few years earlier as an Australian soldier, but that was a war zone; this was magical. Bali was a spellbinding kingdom of the Orient, enhanced by the magic-mushroom omelettes he would share with his tall American friend, Charlie Tonlady, and other friends he had met at Kuta beach – an idyllic, small but popular village where local people would provide accommodation for travellers. They would congregate in and around a sun shelter by the beach and tell incredible stories. The Island of the Gods: a paradise haven for young free-thinking adventurers, blending in an atmosphere of Bohemian joy. Miles had given up on God when he left home, wanting to discover the truth with an open mind, but he still found it difficult to extinguish his Catholic indoctrination. In the army he had been stationed in Townsville prior to being sent to Vietnam and had to state which religion he wanted put on his dog tags. When Miles disclosed that he did not believe in God anymore, the chaplain had said, "You must be a very lonely man, going to where you are going. You may need him". That had hit him and challenged his resolve to find the truth without influence from Western institutions, without prejudice. He was done with blind belief.

Charlie was a hippie from California who supplied dodgy student discount cards for travellers, while Bronwyn and Myfanwy Tickels were two Welsh sisters who were on holiday and had followed Miles over from Darwin after they became close friends at the Top End Folk Club. They would bring glamour to an otherwise grubby ensemble, apart from Loostea, real name Louise Caddy. It was a name Miles had given her in Fannie Bay, a suburb of Darwin. She was very fond of Itchy, the name she had given him. Miles liked to sing, and after being discharged from the army, his brother Piles, a regular singer at the folk club, had inspired him to study traditional folk music and folklore. As a man of the people, he was fascinated by social history, stories of how the ordinary working people of Britain, Ireland and Australia survived in their time when injustice to the people was common, all being told in song. Loostea had also become friends with Itchy at the folk club, an attractive and buxom girl from London who was hoping to travel with him, an option he was open to. *If it happens, it happens*, he had briefly pondered; he was ready for anything.

Then there was Austin Ayphor. He and his pregnant girlfriend were on their way to a Kibbutz in Israel. "Why go there?" said Miles, puffing on a local fag made with cloves that he would not be trying again. He was curious why they should undertake such a journey in her condition.

"Peace, brother, peace... that's why. Live, work and bring up my family in a commune of peace", said Austin. Charlie was blunt when he said, "They have not had peace in that area ever. Biblical times tell you that. It's an ancient hatred between Hebrews and Philistines; it keeps going on and on and on. It is, however, the birthplace of Christianity, so what will you be, Christian or Jew?"

Miles had to join in with, "Isn't it odd... Israel is Jewish and not Catholic. I mean, Jesus was born there. Why is Rome the home of the Pope? And after the Romans crucified him, I am sure there is a very good explanation as to why they are called Roman Catholics. I mean, they used to throw Christians to the lions".

Austin replied, "Religion does not play a major role in the Kibbutz. You can believe what you like – it is about teaching love. It's about working the farm for the collective good of the commune".

"I wish you well," said Charlie.

"I like the idea of a commune", said Miles while thinking, *She is going to have a baby soon. Crikey, they're taking a chance.*

"How are you getting there?" continued Charlie.

"We fly to Calcutta and then travel to Goa in the south. I expect the baby will be arriving about then, so we will see after that how we will continue".

The group were jollyferkating, well into holiday mode, and the two sisters would swan around in their bikinis directing their attention towards Miles, which put Loostea on the defensive. Myfanwy was cosying up to Miles, when a smiling Loostea observed, "Changing your name from Myfanwy Tickels to Myfanwy Zytchalot would be no great improvement".

Laughter broke out all around, but the comment did not bother Myfanwy and she replied, "I am sorry, you are right. It would be going from bad to worse, but who said anything about changing names?"

"My name is pronounced 'Zytchalow'", said Miles. "Not that you lot care. Call me what you like". Everybody was enjoying the banter and adding to the fun, and they were all quite amused with the explanation of why she called Miles "Itchy". Meanwhile, he swanned around in his traditional Balinese sarong, not caring about anything. Then Myfanwy waltzed him off to the beach and a moonlight swim. People came and went with fascinating stories to tell, and he would soon become no stranger to the marijuana that would be passed around. Tales of places to see and cheap places to stay had Miles enthralled, all of which went into his journal.

One day, Miles and Charlie took a bus to see traditional Balinese music and dance, where male dancers would put themselves in a trancelike state and perform with daggers to Gamelan music, an orchestra of gongs. Bali's traditional dance and music were so different. *Balinese and a racket,* at least that is what Miles thought, but Charlie said, "I like that Gamelan music". Only for Miles to return with, "What? you must be stoned! 'If music be the food of love', you better keep the sound down or you will end up on your own!"

Some days were spent on the beach, but on a lot of days, Miles and Charlie would take off in the morning on hired bicycles. They would pedal slowly along in a different direction each day, often stopping to gaze in wonder at the stunning views of the tiered paddy fields. There was so much to see on this picturesque volcanic island. They had stopped for a smoke where a farmer was displaying his artwork of the irrigated layers of rice paddy fields on the mountainsides. It was stunning and Miles purchased a painting from the farmer, who never stopped smiling. The boys found it amusing when the Bali Beach Hotel tour bus would flash by giving rich tourists fleeting glimpses of their culture.

Another day they had taken a local bus with no glass in the windows for a boy to climb in and out and collect fares, with planks of wood stretched across the bus for seating. Miles found it hard to contain his laughter when a lady used the back of Charlie's shirt to wipe her baby's bottom; it was done so nonchalantly and without Charlie knowing. He was not amused when he discovered the stain, and Miles took a photo of Charlie and his shirt next to the bus. *One for the album*, he thought. They had been to see a large Hindu temple and were astonished to see the stone carvings on the temple walls. There was a man on a bicycle, a car… How could that be? These carvings dated back thousands of years. A mystery that nobody could explain.

On another day, they had been cycling on their hired bikes, when they witnessed the ritual cremation of a high priest, outside a Hindu temple to Brahma, God of all knowledge. The flames engulfed a decorative hollowed-out coffin in the shape of a life-size bull, it was a magnificent celebration with people being joyous and happy for the departed. They told Miles death was not to be feared; his time on earth was over and his spirit had moved on and that they were happy for him as he had gone to a better place, gone to join the gods.

Although loving every minute of beautiful Bali, Miles knew the party was over. Loostea could not wait any longer and had gone to Jakarta.

"I have a long way to go, Charlie. I've got to get miles on the road – that is me, Miles, and road miles", he said. "I have got to get serious about this journey and make a start sometime. I really have been here too long".

The next day he had pulled himself together and said, "Charlie, I am not happy with that President Nixon. He just devalued the dollar… my money is now worth ten per cent less. I'm off".

"I reckon so, buddy… your road awaits. You take care, and good luck", Charlie said with a smile. "Send me a Christmas card!"

Miles had picked up the dodgy student's discount card for his travels, and directions of where to go and places to stay. Directions! All he knew was to head west, his quest to follow the sun. He had a small world map showing flight paths on an Air France supplement; this was going to be his guide for this overland trek to Europe, England, and home. A daunting adventure for this young intrepid, and maybe he was a bit naive for a Vietnam war vet. Bali had inspired him to see more of other cultures – curiosity was bursting through his veins, as Bali was so beautifully different.

Miles had been brought up in Whitby, Northeast England. His family, who had strong Catholic convictions, would keep him in constant supply of indoctrination. He had felt shackled by religion, and at nineteen, he was ready to find his own way in the world, to escape, and so he followed his brother Piles (short for Pibald), who had left two years previously by emigrating to work in Australia, and the Melbourne Tramways had sponsored him to do the same. He had always felt a connection with Australia; after all, Captain Cook had sailed from Whitby to discover the promised land, and for a £10 assisted passage, Miles would sail from Southampton on a four-week cruise to Australia, stopping off at Las Palmas in Gran Canaria, then Cape Town in South Africa, where he got his first taste of life.

He had been in a fish and chip shop when a Black man dropped his money on the floor. Miles instinctively went to help the man, only to be vigorously told to leave him be by the shopkeeper. He had heard about Apartheid and now he had first-hand experience that was brutal. The next port of call was Fremantle, in Western Australia, which impressed him so much he vowed to return before finally disembarking in Melbourne to be met by his brother, who had travelled from Sydney to meet him. At the time of leaving home he had been excited to be on his way, but sad to leave behind his ma, pa, and sister, Nobald. It was his time to see the world – he knew there was a different world out there and he was going to find it. Take every day as an adventure and live every moment, for tomorrow it would be a memory. There had been a Mibald in the family going back many years, originating in their homeland, Latvia, and his father knew in later years his name would help in character building and survival, as it had for himself.

Miles had loved Darwin, the extreme climate, being either hot and dry or hot and wet. He had been unusually content. The folk club was important to him, and it attracted people with a variety of stories to tell. The Hippie Trail he had heard about a few times, but it was not until he met Blinky Tom Bowler, an English guy with an unfortunate twitch, that serious interest was employed. Miles met Tom when he joined the Field Density Testing Laboratory in Darwin, where he worked as a laboratory technician, spending weeks at a time testing road samples out in Arnhem land. Miles was already loving life in the bush when his new colleague triggered a different adventure in him, the spiritual one.

Tom had not long arrived in Darwin after he had travelled overland from Europe, but he was emotionally upset, as his girlfriend had just left him after their amazing journey together. He spoke of Buddhism and showed Miles how, in the evening, he would squat in the lotus position, meditating, which he had picked up from his time in Thailand. He had also told Miles that Buddhism was a religion of no-religion – there was no God – and that one needed to understand the impermanence of life, that life kept changing. In doing so, you could find liberation from suffering. The Buddha taught of how to guide you on your path, but each person's journey was their own. Life changed all the time; if the mind could absorb this truth, one could accept suffering, learn from it, and move on. The past could not be changed, so one must let go of what was behind them and focus on the truth of the moment, and of what lay ahead. The secret was to accept what had happened and live for today, but that was easier said than done. After all he had said, Tom was still finding it hard but had many a tale to tell and his stories really struck a chord of beautiful music with Miles.

Wow. Here he was in Darwin, the perfect starting point. Why not? *I can do that*, he thought. *I can overland it back to England, see the folks, then return to this wonderful and challenging land that is so me.* So, without much thought about the dangers of such a venture, he started getting his things together, like passport, vaccinations, journal, camera, rucksack, travellers' cheques and a ticket to Bali.

"Have you got everything you need, like enough money?" asked Piles, who had tried to warn Miles about travelling alone and who was quite apprehensive about the trip continuing.

"You are coming back, aren't you? You're an Australian now."

"Of course I'll be back. This is like leaving home. Did you know Loostea has already gone? I am to meet up with her in Bali. I won't be alone. I will just have to be careful with the money. I've got a thousand US dollars in travellers' cheques and I'm going on an adventure, but I'll be back when the stone stops rolling", laughed Miles.

Piles said, "I am not sure about you taking just US money; I have heard rumblings over there in the US. And watch out for that Loostea… she is up to something, and she's got you in her sights. Well, have a good trip and don't freak out Ma and Pa when you get home. Good luck. And write!"

Piles knew Ma and Pa would find a different boy now. How would they handle it? And would the trip cure his brother's wanderlust?

The bus was ready to move out again, and after his embarrassment had diminished Miles went back to chatting with the passengers, proud to be on his own and able to identify with the people. They were all keen to practice what English they could, and many a funny conversation took place with Miles replying in broken Malay. It was fun, as they all got on extremely well. He soon realised the rucksack he was carrying was too big and he would need to travel lighter, but for the time being he would have to carry on. The bus journey through Java was much the same and once he arrived in Jakarta, he knew there was no turning back. He had ferried over from Bali to Java and a bus took him to Surabaya. Then it was onto a steam train to Jogja, where he had wanted to buy a Batik sarong, before continuing on to Jakarta. He had been wearing a sarong since arriving in Bali, loving the freedom and comfort, ideal in such a warm climate, but he decided to make the one he had suffice and save the money.

When he was in Jakarta, he wondered if Loostea was still there and why she had to go when she did. Jakarta was heaving with people and traffic, and he took no time to find the bus to take him to Merak away from the melee. From there he slept on the ferry to Sumatra, a name he remembered from his school days that even then had conjured up a fascination for the Orient. A steam train then took him to Palembang, and from there another train took him to Lubuk linggau, before he hopped onto the bus he was on, that would take him to Padang. This was a fun and absorbing journey for Miles, as he was now on a bus, in the jungle with the insects biting. It was the wet season, and the jungle road was mud and more mud. He was embracing every moment being with the people. In '69 to '70, he had spent twelve months in the Vietnam jungle, and this was no hardship for him; rather, it was enjoyable, knowing nobody was out to shoot him. Monsoon rain was impeding their progress and when faced with a very steep hill, it was all passengers off: The bus was sliding in the mud… as were the passengers trying to push it. A stake was driven in the ground halfway up the hill and a chain attached to the stake and the axle. The bus then pulled itself up as the chain wrapped itself around the axle. This, of course, had a devastating effect on the axle, and when on the next and last attempt to advance up the hill, the axle broke. The passengers were not happy. The bus was going nowhere; they had to stay on the bus in the jungle until the bus was fixed. But Miles loved every minute of being in the bus he was on top of the bus… he had pushed the bus and pulled the bus, walked beside and behind the bus and loved every moment.

The rain prevented a fire being built and people were grumpy, then Miles started to sing "Old MacDonald Had a Farm". It had an easy chorus of "E-I-E-I-O", and with some encouragement, it was not long before everybody was joining in. "E-I-E-I-O! And on that farm, he had a pig, E-I-E-I-O! With a grunt, grunt here, and a grunt, grunt there, here a grunt, there a grunt, everywhere a grunt, grunt. Old MacDonald had a farm, E-I-E-I-O!" Howls of laughter broke out with the grunting pigs, when somebody said, "That should keep the tigers away!" When Miles had gone through the farm animals, the passengers shared what food there was, and Miles thought, *This is beautiful.* What joy it was to hear fun and laughter in a dark wet jungle, quite different to his experience in the Vietnam jungle.

Amazingly, a new axle was fitted to the bus in the extreme conditions and when they finally arrived at their destination, they were all one big happy family. Miles was invited to stay with many of the passengers, for this had been an adventure for everyone on board. The trip had taken three days to cover just three hundred and fifty miles, and they had all bonded after an incredible bus journey. "Must have a group photo", said Miles, but it was hard finding someone to take the picture as everybody wanted to be in it.

His next stop was Lake Toba, and he had to take the bus to Parapat which left in the morning, so the invitation from Tukka Phuka was graciously accepted. He enjoyed wonderful hospitality, and he was refreshed as he climbed on the bus the next day, prepared for whatever the day would bring, on his continuing adventure. Parapat was where you could ferry over to the island on Lake Toba, a must-visit on the Hippie Trail. He had learned the lake was a volcanic crater and on boarding the ferry he could see an enchanting *Batak* house with its curved fascia and decorative tiles. It was a short trip over and on landing, he instinctively headed for the house he had seen. There, he was greeted by an interesting array of well-travelled hippies, all eager to impress new travellers. Soon it was as if they all were old friends. Miles was happy during the exciting conversations, as he was able to contribute his own tales, and when he enquired with, "Hey, where is the toilet?" he was greeted with laughter as they pointed him in the right direction. At the back of the house, there was a pit with a straining post at the top to hold on to; this was vital, as a sheet of corrugated iron served as a chute down into the pit, where two black pigs lay in wait, eager to scramble up the chute for the offerings dispatched. This was not for the faint-hearted; this was wild. They were all laughing on his return, knowing what he had just experienced.

At mealtime, everybody would squat in a circle in the centre of the floor, away from their sleeping spaces by the walls of this ornately decorated and spacious house. They would eat delicious, life-enhancing, banana *susu* – bananas and condensed milk. It was instant energy. They would smoke weed, swap stories and tell tales of places to see and stay. This was a delight, and it all went down into the journal; it was as entertaining as it was of benefit. After all, this is how he came to be at Lake Toba, by listening, with a zest for knowledge and adventure. Miles did not want to leave. Everybody had wonderful and unusual stories to tell, but they too had to move on; it was like a meeting of wandering souls, each embracing the moment together. Tomorrow it would be a memory. He left Lake Toba after taking a group photo and one of the pigs in the pit, with lots of addresses in his journal of places to stay and things to do and see.

A bus took him from Parapat to Medan at the top end of Sumatra, where he shared a room with an Australian called Valentine Anweir. The journal was becoming invaluable. The accommodation was for travellers sharing rooms, but people were reluctant to share with Valentine as he was down sick with hepatitis. This would not be uncommon in a part of the world with questionable sanitary conditions. *What is the worst that can happen? He needs help*, thought Miles.

"Valentine Anweir", the Australian said meekly, introducing himself.

"I come from there", said Miles, grinning, "Valen Tyne *and Wear*, North of England, and it's where I am heading. How are you? How can I help?" Valentine was a sick-looking hippie collapsed on his bed.

"Hepatitis. I need medicine", he replied with difficulty.

"I will go see what I can find. Now, don't go away", said Miles, "I will try not to be too long", as he left for the *Apotik* to get some medication for him. Miles was still on a high from the bus journey and the wonderful Lake Toba as he strolled along in the heat of the day, loving every minute. At the *Apotik* he was instantly attracting attention, being a European with blond hair, when an attractive young girl came over, smiling, eyes all aflutter. He told her of Valentine's plight and asked if she could help. Off she went and came back with a large tin of glucose.

"You come back tomorrow, we make up medicine for you", said the young lady. "My name is Lusti", she added, as she continued to ask many questions.

Miles was polite to the attractive Lusti and told her he would come back the following day. Valentine had turned yellow and was looking extremely ill; he was going to need to return to Australia soon, but he was too weak and needed to recover well enough before making the journey.

The following day Miles went to the *Apotik* to collect the medicine, only to be greeted by giggling girls who all wanted to serve him. The lovely Lusti who had served him the day before came over with the medicine, shooing the other girls away. She was all over him like a rash and asked where he lived, saying she would call around to help. He was taken by this exotic beauty, and they talked for a long time before he thanked her and headed back with the magic potion. When he opened the package there was a note from Lusti, which read:

Mr Miles,

You very handsome. When you come to England, you must write a letter to me! When will we meet again, Mr Miles? Where could I see you again, Mr Miles? Maybe in dream, sweet dream? Sweet your smile, sweet your beautiful eyes.

Wow, I made an impression there. *How lovely is that?* he thought, as he prepared the liver-cleansing compound.

"Val, is there any more I can do? Anything, as I'll be heading to Penang soon."

"There is", said Val. "If you can take this parcel with you and deliver it to Sun Tin Wong in Chulia Street, Georgetown. That's on Penang Island. You can stay there as he has an accommodation area, very cheap."

Miles said, "Is there anything dodgy in the parcel?"

"Oh, not really. Just some dried magic mushroom soup powder. He and his brother have a reputation for the best soup in Penang", whispered Val, hardly able to speak. "There should be no trouble."

Miles looked at the package. It was the size of a book, weighed and felt like one, and was inside a maroon velvet bag tied with a yellow ribbon, adding further mystery. He put it in his rucksack, without being too convinced of the contents.

It was a short flight in a short plane to Penang Island and a checkpoint.

"Now then", said the customs man as Miles was about to go through the gates. *This is not supposed to happen*, he mused, until he realised, he was travelling from Indonesia into Malaysia. "May I see your passport?" said the official.

Miles clumsily passed over his passport and the official smiled as he read aloud "My balls itch a lot."

"So do mine," said one of the passengers, and the people around them began to laugh. "No, no, sir. It's pronounced Zytchalow, Mibald Zytchalow. Zytchalow!" cried Miles. *Here we go again*, he thought. This was not the first time he had encountered similar situations, which generally ended up with everyone smiling. And so it was, as Miles was ushered on amid the laughter by the smiling official.

Chapter Two

Malaysia

When he was in the army, everybody knew Miles; on his first roll call in recruit training, the sergeant called out, "My Balls Itch a Lot?" All ranks were unable to suppress their laughter, through which Miles cried "Zytchalow, Sergeant. Zytchalow!"

"Quiet in the ranks!" shouted the sergeant. "You will speak when spoken to. Is that clear, you itchy-balled Pommie?"

"Yes, Sergeant", was the meek reply. Miles had been in Australia only six months, and was living in Perth, when he received his call-up papers for national service. The call-up was done by a lottery of birth dates and that was when Miles's balls dropped. He remembered what the aggrieved official told him after just arriving in Melbourne to work as a tram conductor: *"This country does not need the likes of you"*. Miles had at once realised the job was not for him and resigned after just two days. The tramways official was rightly annoyed, but now was the time Miles could show his commitment, and he vowed to prove the official wrong.

He had left Melbourne after working in an abattoir in Footscray to afford to travel overland to Perth, sharing the cost of the petrol with four other guys; it was across the hot, dusty and corrugated Nullarbor plain, in a Holden station wagon, that he had spent his first Christmas away from home. This was a massive contrast to the way Christmas had been for him, and it was all part of the adventure.

Now, there was the prospect of army life. He deliberated on what to do, which did not take long as he had nothing better to do. He was sharing a ramshackle old house with five other guys who would party every week, life was a lot of fun. He would often go down to Albany where he had worked in the wool stores and on the railway but now was the time to put some direction in his life. He had considered the possibility of being sent to Vietnam but that interested him also. *I would be an Australian, one of the people.* He underwent ten weeks of recruit training, integrating and bonding with his new countrymen and comrades. He was proud when marching in the passing-out parade but sad nobody was there for him on his day of achievement. After the cold of State Victoria, he was posted to the 6RAR Battalion in the tropical climate of Townsville in Queensland, where his name arrived before he did. He was called many names, and he was the brunt of many a joke. Most times he would just ignore or smile the jesting away. It was strange that he got called "Zitch" by his platoon mates – the only time he had ever had that handle. His sergeant was an Englishman called Stu Pidamnot, who took Miles under his wing. He was telling him about being a Buffalo. A society whose meetings were held in secret up at the lodge.

"Is it a religion? Or like the Masons?" Miles asked, interrupting his sergeant.

"Not quite", was his reply. "Similar, but we do not speak about religion. It is like being in the army; you get to know lots of people and create a common bond. You look after each other".

From the airport, Miles took a bus into Georgetown, and he made his way to Chulia Street. There was a strong Chinese connection on this Malayan Island, integrating easily into the crowded narrow streets: exotic smells of the Orient mixed with the hustle and bustle, instantly filling him with wonder and fascination, but he was beginning to feel unwell. He asked someone if they knew Sun Tin Wong and was directed to a shop with accommodation above. A section of floor with a mattress and body pillow was the accommodation on offer and Miles soon found a space in this popular and cheap travellers' rest.

He looked around and thought he spotted Loostea. It was. She was overjoyed when she saw him and bounded over, crying, "Itchy, Itchy! Oh, Miles". Flinging her arms around him, she squealed with excitement, "How are you? You tell me everything".

He sang to her, "Hey, haaaang on, Loostea, Loostea, hang on! How long you been here?"

"Oh, I just arrived. How are you?" a bubbling Loostea replied. "Did you get through customs alright?"

"Yes", said Miles, wondering why she should ask such a question. "Bit of a commotion with my name, but I expect that".

"I thought you might pass through okay. You're looking a bit off-colour", Loostea said.

"Well, quite frankly, I don't feel at all well, and I know it sounds funny, but I'm looking for Sun Tin Wong".

"Well, you got something *wong*. I've been chatting with Sing Song… he will help", said Loostea.

He found it hard to even smile when he said, "Not Sing Song Wong", as he was feeling weaker by the minute.

"You best get yourself checked out. What do you want with Sun Tin"? an inquisitive Loostea asked.

"I have a parcel for him from a friend of mine in Sumatra", said Miles.

"That's interesting", she replied.

The next day, Miles was a lot worse, feeling very weak. *Oh, crikey*, he thought. *This is the end*. He forced himself off his mattress on the floor and made his way down to the street below, where he climbed into a *becak* and said, "Hospital".

There were enormous queues; the first was the queue for a number to see the doctor. He was issued number 138. *Oh my god*, he thought, *I'm done for*, as he joined the second queue. He was so weak he could not even sit and had to lie down on the ground and wait. A kind man who had watched Miles in such distress came over and looked at his ticket. He swapped it for a ticket that saw Miles go in next. He wanted to thank the man for his kindness but was in a near state of collapse.

The doctor knew immediately what was wrong: hepatitis. The doctor's dilemma was to give priority to local people. Miles was thinking, *I'm a foreigner; I am definitely done for*. On attempting to move Miles on, he vomited and collapsed. The doctor had no choice but to put Miles in a ward. For seven days, Miles was in another world, being woken up to take medication before drifting back into oblivion.

When Miles had not returned that day, Loostea went looking for him, starting at the hospital. She was happy to find him being cared for and in the best place, then returned later with his rucksack to put under the bed. When conscious, Miles would let his mind wander. This was the worst that could have happened. He would think of Val and of how he would recover without the care that Miles was receiving. Maybe the compound Lusti made up would encourage his recovery. Doubts began to creep in about continuing, but where would he go? He could only go back to Australia, and the embarrassment that would mean… No, he would keep going and focus on survival. He felt weak, but he was also getting better every day. Being forever the optimist, he would not be downhearted; even though he had lost a lot of weight in such a short time, he would stay positive.

"You balls itchy?" said the nurse, as Miles looked up to see a vision of loveliness, an angel of mercy with his medication.

"Have I died?" said Miles, as he admired this creature of divine beauty looking over him. During his illness he had turned yellow and only for his blond hair, he could have passed for Bruce Lee. "You call me what you like. What do I call you?" said Miles.

"I am Princess Ketchup Indapie. Now, sit up and take your pills", she said with a glint in her eye.

"I will call you Saucy. Are you a real princess?" asked Miles

"Oh, yes", she said, "and I like go England. You take me, yes?"

"Am I going to live?" said Miles.

"You be fine, very soon. I look after you. You take me with you, yes?" pleaded the princess.

He began to wonder about the lovely princess. She knew a lot about him…how? *I must find out.* Although Miles was still weak, he was certainly improving by the day, but he was going to need to be patient. *A patient with patience*, he thought, as he closed his eyes and drifted off again. Each time he woke from his unconsciousness, he felt stronger. The man in the next bed introduced himself as Chua Fat Long. He was a kind, elderly local man, and he explained the hospital structure. They had three wards: A, B and Free.

Miles had somehow landed in the free ward. He had been in and out of consciousness and there were times when, awake, he witnessed death in the poor man's ward. The last thing the old man opposite did was fall out of bed; he was put on a trolley and covered with a wooden box. A procedure that was carried out with dignity and respect. On another occasion a young boy had passed away, with his family at the bedside, just two beds away from Miles. The crying and wailing was piercing and created such intense emotion that everybody felt the pain of their sorrow, as tears flowed around the ward. *One has to live each day as his last*, he pondered. *Young or old, you just don't know when it is your turn.*

The next time Miles awoke from his recuperating slumber, he said to himself, *Loostea, what is she up to? It must be her telling the princess about me.* She had been calling in every day, even when he was not conscious. *It has to be her, but what is she up to?* He was happy with himself and his deductions when Loostea came to visit.

"Well, you look a lot better", she said with a jangle in her voice, as she sat down beside the bed. She looked him in his yellow eyes, and said, "I am ready to move on, but I will wait for you to get better if you want".

"That may take some time", he told her. "I can only move on when I feel well enough to travel… whenever that may be, who can tell?" Miles began to explain the anxieties he had about his health in an attempt to dissuade her from staying. He told her he needed time to recuperate and build up strength. He was curious about what she was holding back, but he was fond of Loostea and she was very fond of him. He did not want to upset her but urged her to carry on and they could meet up again later. Miles was unaware that Loostea had slipped something into his rucksack while he was talking that would confuse him when it appeared later in the afternoon.

She gave him her London address and said, "Please, look me up as soon as you set foot in England. It is important, promise me. I know you will make it; I'll be waiting for you".

So, Loostea was on her way again and he looked forward to them meeting up back in the UK, as she was very convincingly concerned. Sun Tin Wong came in and introduced himself. He wished Miles a speedy recovery and asked about the parcel.

"It is under the bed, in the rucksack", said Miles, and Sun Tin reached in.

"Someting wong", said Sun Tin Wong. "This not right parcel". He reached in again and pulled out a similar parcel, declaring it to be the right one. Confusion was etched across Miles's face, as he would then introduce him to his new friend in the next bed.

"This is Chua Fat Long, Sun Tin Wong", went the introduction, forcing Miles to suppress a smile. He had met so many new and different friends. Chua Fat and Sun Tin were interested in the journey that Miles was taking, telling him he was very brave, something Miles had not even considered. Each person he met placed their own influence on a willing student of life.

"I have a long way to go, but I have plenty of time. I just got to get better", he was telling Chua Fat and Sun Tin. After Sun Tin Wong left, he looked at the parcel; it was the same. *That's odd*, he thought. *What is going on? Where did the other parcel come from? Loostea, could she be involved in something here? I will ask Sing Song.*

Two weeks in hospital went by, and the doctor felt he was strong enough to recuperate elsewhere. Chua Fat Long had offered to put him up for a few days while Princess Ketchup Indapie wanted to put him up permanent. His best course of action was to go back and see Sun Tin Wong.

"Hello, you, Mr Itchy Balls. You feel better?" said Sing Song, a small corpulent man with a happy exterior. "We keep space for you."

"Thank you, Sing Song. I see you have been talking to Loostea. I feel much better. Need to rest for a while and get rid of this rucksack; I could do with a smaller bag. Can you help?" Miles asked.

"Sing Song have bag made for you. My friend, Foo Ling Yu, he make very cheap. Anything you want, I get. Come, we go see my friend."

"Wait, just one minute. Before we go, tell me about the parcel."

Sing Song stuttered, "O-oh, I know nothing. Loostea ask me to help you. She say keep parcel safe. Come, we go see my friend".

Loostea, of course... what is she up to? And what did Sun Tin Wong take away with him? Well, Sing Song seems to be eager to help. Miles pondered on these thoughts and decided to let Sing Song do what he had been asked to do and see what happened. *I mean what is the worst that can happen? Then again, I've said that before*, he reminded himself.

It was down the street on the left: Choo Sing Shoes next to Choo Hin Gum, the dentist. Foo Ling Yu worked in the tailors at the back; you could have anything you wanted made within twenty-four hours. Sing Song had a pocket sewn onto the base, inside the bag where the velvet parcel would fit. He showed Miles the pocket and what it was for. "Leave parcel in pocket and forget it is there. Loostea say so".

What has she got in there? It felt like a book. *Oh, well, what is the worst that can happen?*

Foo Ling Yu was cheap, so he had a smart shirt, and trousers made to measure cheap also. Even cheaper were the shorts and vest made from flour bags. The travel bag was ideal, and so he then posted his rucksack to England by sea mail and hoped he would arrive home first, before the rucksack, as he had not told his parents he was heading home.

After a few days he had his kit together and he was travelling light as he went just a short way to Batu Ferringhi, where he spent most of his time on the beach and in the water. The sea was warm, like taking a bath, as he focused on building up strength. He had been advised on what to eat and what not to eat – rice and dried fish with no alcohol or oily food, that was it. He had not had beer since leaving Darwin, so no alcohol would not be a problem, and he had developed a taste for dried fish. While he enjoyed the convalescence, he was quickly regaining strength and would soon be able to crack on.

Batu Ferringhi was a small fisherman's village and Sing Song had told Miles to stay at Baba House, owned by a friend of his, where his bag would be safe while he swam in the warm waters. It was peaceful and serene and he had once again found himself in Shangri-la and didn't want to leave. He would read about Malaysian history and culture, in between his swims to get fit.

Sing Song was on the alert when he spotted the Hat, a Chinese pursuant that Loostea had warned him about. He was talking to Sun Tin and when he left, Sing Song went over to find out what he had to say. When Sing Song prompted his brother, he replied, "He ask about Itchy Balls, where he go. I tell him nothing. He dodgy, me no like". Sing Song went around to his friend Foo Ling Yu and they both drove to Batu Ferringhi in the communal van. On arriving, they could see the Hat advancing on Baba House. Miles was having a swim and the Hat's number two, who looked a large figure next to the diminutive Hat, was keeping watch behind a palm tree. Sing Song began to approach Baba House, which made the Hat stop and take a step backwards beside the fishing boat on stilts next to the house. Foo Ling Yu had circled unseen and knocked away the stilts. The boat fell on the Hat, knocking him out and out of sight. His number two came running over as Sing Song and Foo Ling Yu were trying to lift the boat. He pulled him clear, but the Hat was unconscious.

"Bad accident", said Sing Song. "We take him to hospital. Help put him in van." They carried him to the van and off to hospital they went before Miles returned, wondering what happened to the boat.

Each day Miles felt himself getting stronger, and then one morning, he felt good enough to continue. So, without thinking too hard, he decided to hitchhike to Kuala Lumpur. He took a bus out of Georgetown to mainland Penang. As it went over the bridge, he felt like he was leaving home. He had felt safe, they had cared for him and made him well, he had been shown kindness and compassion by the local people, he had made friends, they were in his heart. Miles was unaware he was being watched, even on the beach, and on the bus, he was being watched by two suspicious characters on a motorbike wearing sunglasses, and one with his arm in a sling and wearing a distinctively colourful hat. Singapore didn't look far away on his world map and Singapore was the place he wanted to visit; it meant going South instead of North, but back in his army days, he had declined the offer to sign on for another three years even though the battalion was due to be posted to Singapore. Sergeant Stu Pidamnot had told him to beware when in Bugis Street and he wanted to see what he meant.

When will I be this way again? he thought. *It's only an inch on the map and I have the time… little money, but time.* So, it was off the bus and out onto the road, sticking out his thumb and a car stopped right away. Miles looked every bit the foreign traveller as a few vehicles slowed down to pick him up, causing the following motorcycle to swerve clumsily. He could have had his pick of rides. *These people are wonderful… I could live here*, he thought, *but the road awaits.*

Each driver along the route was inquisitive, and Miles was just as keen to chat. He enjoyed learning of the Malay culture from the people who lived there, mainly Muslims. Everybody he had met was friendly and willing to help in any way they could. They had clawed him away from the jaws of death... well, that's how it felt to him, a stranger, a foreigner, and now he was entering Kuala Lumpur with Singapore in his sights.

After wandering around the attractions of Kuala Lumpur asking questions, he got word of the newspaper van's regular trip to Johar Baru, and it left in the early hours of the morning. Miles was unaware of the two men on a motorbike who were intent on taking his bag; they had followed Miles waiting for the opportunity to seize it. They thought it had arrived, when speeding towards their quarry they skidded on an oil spill after somebody knocked over a drum of oil in front of them, taking them across the road and under a parked truck and completely out of view. That somebody was Valentine Anweir; he had recovered in Medan, thanks to the care he received from Lusti, and followed the route Miles would have taken. He was concerned about the safety of the parcel, and he flew to Penang and went straight to see Sun Tin Wong.

Valentine would often visit Penang and Bali in his capacity as a freelance reporter for holiday magazines in New Zealand and had known the brothers for some years. Over a bowl of their special mushroom soup, Val heard of Sing Song's heroics and was so pleased with him, he gave him a hug and made him blush. The helpful Sing Song was going to take him to Batu Ferringhi in the van when they saw Miles climb onto a bus. More of a concern was seeing the Hat, with his arm in a sling, sitting pillion on a motorbike close behind.

"We must follow. Are you with me, Sing Song?" Val said hastily.

"You bet. Let's go, boss. Sing Song good detective, like Charlie Chan."

They followed the Hat to Kuala Lumpur and saw what was about to happen, when Val acted to avert the danger. Totally unaware of what had happened about him, Miles sauntered along until he found the depot, paid six dollars to the driver and climbed into the back of the newspaper van, waking up a few hours later at the Johar depot. A short bus journey took him into Singapore, where he found himself a cheap hotel and then went walkabouts. Apartment blocks like stacks of dominos caught the eye – a prominent feature, as they also appeared on the Singapore dollar note. After a few hours just meandering about, he came to Bugis Street. People were being waited on at the tables that were spread around the street, music was sounding, and people were partying, but the spectacle – or freak show – were the beautiful women parading around. However, they were not women at all. *Oh my goodness,* this was freaky. Miles had not encountered anything like this before: pretty men dressed as women. Again, something new and another weird experience… *let's stack them up and crack on!*

The next day he was heading out of Singapore hitchhiking up the east coast of Malaysia, hoping to see the turtles on the beach and spend the night there. It was slow going, as the lifts he got were only short trips, until, after a lift on the back of a lorry, he found himself in a village on the edge of the jungle. He did not know where he was as he walked apprehensively past the low timber dwellings each side of the road, with the last being open-fronted and lit up. He slowed down to a shuffle and could see there was a party going on; the music was clear to hear as he headed up the road going out and into the jungle.

"Stop!" was the cry from a man at the party. "Tigers, tigers, you stay in village. I fix you place to stay. No go jungle. Tigers. Come in, you be safe here. First, you must have drink." He was clearly concerned for this stranger heading into the jungle at night and passed him a beer. Miles tried in vain to explain why he could not have a beer, extending his thanks for the kindness, but in the end, he smiled, felt guilty and sipped his beer, unable to refuse.

His saviour introduced himself as Kharma Dazeahed. He and his family were having a celebration with the news his wife, Sutra, was expecting a baby. Miles was now quite at home, conversing well enough for everyone to understand and enjoyed the banter, but it was late, and he was beginning to feel weak again. Kharma had been chatting with Miles all evening and noticed his decline.

"Come", he said, "I'll show you where you sleep". He was shown to a house across the road and to a small room with three sets of bunk beds, on which he sat on the bed nearest to him, rolled over and collapsed. Kharma smiled as he put his bag under the bed and placed a cover over him before closing the mosquito net, saying, "Sleep well". Sleep well, he did, till early afternoon the next day, waking to the sound of children chattering beside his bed. In came Sutra, gesturing to Miles to arise and join them to eat. He arose to the spicy aromas that floated through and made him realise how hungry he was. Good sign, he thought. The food was glorious, and they talked for a long time with everybody eager to speak. Realising it was too late to start out again, it was Kharma who received an approving nod when suggesting Miles stay another night to be fit and well in the morning. He was grateful, for in the morning he felt better than ever; the extra rest had thoroughly refreshed him, and he was ready for whatever lay ahead.

With everybody smiling, they waved him on his way, as into the jungle he strode with renewed vigour and cooked rice wrapped in a leaf given him by Sutra. One lift took him to Pasir Mas and a train took him over the border and into Thailand. He had been advised way back in Bali that when crossing borders you need to look like a tourist. Miles had changed from his travelling clothes and into the nice shirt and pants Foo Ling Yu had made just for the purpose of crossing the border. A customs man came through the carriage, checking people's papers. The customs man was aware of this ruse when asking Miles for his passport. He read out, "'My Balls Itch a Lot', let me see your bag". As he looked through the bag, Miles did well to keep the parcel undetected and felt the change of clothing had no effect at all; however, everything was fine, and the train moved on and finally reached Bangkok.

After enjoying so much of the rural countryside, this was a different scenario: a busy, bustling city, it was a huge contrast to the peace and calm of the unspoilt and spectacular countryside. He had no plans to stay long in the city and wanted to go north to Chiang Mai. A city where Blinky Tom had told him he could learn more about the people and culture. His journal had him looking for Rama IV Road and it was easy to find as it was the main drag, resembling a racetrack, with no slowing down the fast-moving traffic. He found the cheap hotel room above the cafe shown in detail in his journal, and this is where he met Andy Kister, a smart and casually dressed English guy who was eating in the cafe below. The seedy hotel was owned by the chef, Ahphor Phucsake. It was always active with young girls circulating, looking for business, and with the aromatic steam from the busy wok enhancing the atmosphere, it was magic. Andy was from Brighton on the south coast of England, and he was there as a holiday tour operator, enjoying the delights that Bangkok had to offer.

Miles had been to Bangkok, three years before, when on six days R&R from Vietnam. He had seen many sights in those six days. All the usual tourist attractions had been explored, taken to by the taxi he had hired for his stay. He had completed six months of duty in Vietnam and had another six months to serve; he was wild, not knowing if he would survive the rest of the tour. He had teamed up with an American soul brother he met on the flight from Saigon to Bangkok, with whom he shared the cost of the taxi. The taxi driver was also their guide and took them to a flash hotel, where they booked in and changed out of uniform, before taking them to a massage parlour, where two delightful ladies kept them company on their six days' leave. It was an unusual friendship, as the soul brothers generally kept to themselves. The soul brother had introduced himself as Delicious Dawson from Delaware, but Miles called him Deli. The accommodating taxi driver had supplied them with plenty of grass and Miles and Deli were stoned most of the time they were there. When Deli took Miles to an American bar full of soul brothers, there were instant bad feeling towards Deli for being with a white guy. This did not bother Deli as he and Miles danced together, for a laugh that really upset the others.

Deli said to Miles, "I am my own man – a Black man – but I don't go with all we are fed by the newspapers".

Miles queried, "But you guys have had it hard, and still do. Is there a cultural revolution going on?"

"Oh, yeah, it has been a long time coming, and it could take a long time for old wounds to heal and prejudice to disappear. It all comes down to how you teach your children. Teach the children well, and armed with good knowledge, there will be good change…there must be change, there will be change, make no mistake. The world is changing all the time; change is inevitable…who knows, there might be a Black president one day".

Miles had a tattoo done on his arm by an old man who looked like Ho Chi Min: an image of a butterfly and dove with a peace scroll. He had seen cock fighting, crocodiles and snakes; he even had a python placed around his neck. But now he was on a cultural, spiritual mission and wanted to visit Northern Thailand.

The city was alive when Andy and Miles went exploring and came across a British ex-pats club, saving them from the constant mayhem abounding around them. They had taken a ride in a three-wheeled Lambretta taxi that was death-defying madness, weaving in and out of traffic at breakneck speed. But although it was nerve-wracking, Miles loved it.

"I think we will walk back", said a shaken Andy, as they climbed out into the bright lights and scantily clad girls dancing to the music from the open-fronted bars. They spotted The Bulldog Club and ventured over; it was a club that had a quality about it. The ladies were high-class and did not bother you unless you wanted them to. There was a dart board being used, giving that English feel for the selective clientele of this sanctuary. They got chatting to Beau Narrow, a journalist who, seven years before, had stopped off on his way to Australia, then realising he was in Shangri-la, he stayed. He was able to tell Miles about visas, and that no travel visas were being issued for Burma unless you had a flight ticket back out. This was a blow for Miles as he had hoped to cross into Burma up north. This meant with no visa for Burma, he would have to fly to Calcutta. He was still going up north to experience the true Thai culture and come back through Laos. Beau was able to help a lot with his knowledge of travel in and around Thailand, having had to renew his visa in Laos every three months until recently.

Miles was still not fit and said, "Now don't be cross, Beau", which got some jeering and groans. "Sorry, could not resist the pun." He went on to explain why he was only drinking soda water, but he kept a cheerful presence; he did not want to spoil an evening of gathering information in such a comfortable environment.

A mystical lady known as Madame Pistake used Miles's camera to take a picture of them and then performed her palm reading on the guests. She took Miles's right palm and gasped, "You are a free spirit, a special one. I see the *M*. You are protected…do not fear the road". She reluctantly let go of his hand. She had felt an energy, a high vibration and wanted to know more, but they were all leaving and wished each other good luck and happy travels, as she was left contemplating what perils Miles had in front of him.

Miles and Andy strolled back up town. "See you for breakfast", said Andy as they parted to their quite different hotels. Miles entered through the open-fronted cafe, and headed to a staircase at the rear leading to the rooms above. The secret was to get into his room before being accosted by ladies who would appear from nowhere. He did not know the secret, and just when he thought he was safe, a foot was in the door.

"*Didi Mau*, I have no money", he would cry. "*Me Uc Dai Loi*, me cheap Charlie, go away." But after exhausting exchanges, he would relent and open the door.

In the morning, Miles came down. He could see Ahphor Phucsake through the steam, tossing the contents of the wok in the kitchen area by the cafe entrance. The smells and steam drifted out into the street as Andy walked in. Over breakfast they talked a lot about travelling, which got Andy intrigued about the unplanned journey that he realised the fearless Miles was undertaking.

"I have these embassy addresses I got off Beau last night, so I'll get my visas sorted today and check out the bus for Chiang Mai", said Miles.

"Hey, listen", an excited Andy spoke with concerned tones. "I will need to know how you get on. Here is my card. Look me up when you get back; I might be able to help you out."

They met up again that evening and over a meal of spicy meat and rice, Miles spoke of his visits to the embassies and that he now had travel visas for Laos and India. A young lady came over to clear away the bowls and Miles asked her what they had eaten as it was very nice.

"Dog" was the reply.

An aghast look fell upon their faces as Miles spluttered, "I am going to see if I can get to my room unscathed as I have to be up early to catch the bus for Chiang Mai. So, I will say goodbye now and all being well, I'll see you in the UK". They shook hands and Miles dodged his way to his room like a bear being chased by honeybees.

Chapter Three

---ᴄⱴᴐ---

Thailand

He had heard a lot about Chiang Mai, from Blinky Tom in Darwin, who had embraced the culture, and told of the inner peace that could be found through Buddhism. They stopped at a roadhouse for food and Miles's technique for consuming rice fast would sustain him on the long but pleasant journey, where he would continue to engage with the people.

There was a man on the bus he thought he had seen before, not so much the man, but the hat; he had seen that hat before. On arrival in Chiang Mai, he once again began to feel unwell. He took out his trusty journal to find a cheap hotel, which was located next to a temple. He found it with no trouble and was surprised to see it did not look too bad. He checked in and went straight to his room, left his bags on the bed and made an urgent dash to the shared washroom. He made the washroom just in time. *Wow,* he thought. *What caused that? I know, it was the dog.* In his haste to make it to the washroom, he had left his room door open, and on his return, he found his belongings disturbed His bag had been opened and emptied onto the bed: his camera was gone.

Oh crikey, he groaned. It had to be an opportunist move from the room across the landing; they had their door open when he made his dash. *I'll have to be more careful. But when you gotta go, you gotta go.*

They could not of had much time, he thought, and the parcel was still in its concealed pocket that had now proved to have been a wise move. He went to close the door, and that is when he saw the Hat, knocking on the door of the room Miles suspected.

I better keep my eye on him, he thought. He was regretting the loss of the camera and the pictures it held. He tried to think positive. *Less weight to carry*, was his only comforting thought.

There were many Buddhist temples in Chiang Mai, each with their own splendour. Pictures of the king adorned most buildings, and you could feel this compliment of loyalty to the king and the spirituality of Buddhism. Hundreds of steps led up to an obviously popular temple with many devotees making the climb. What surprised Miles were the many stalls displaying souvenirs and trinkets lining the start to the ascent. The six-inch wooden carvings of a man in a barrel stood out amongst the other trinkets on display; Miles could not contain his curiosity when he picked one up and lifted the barrel. He was startled, then he laughed, as an oversized penis sprang up. Not expecting such an item for sale on the way to a holy shrine, he had to find out why. He was informed by the local guide, a man called Ugli Twat who was dressed in traditional Thai formal costume, that it began as a protest by an important native man, Upya Gonga, against the American colonisers in the 1900s, for disturbing their way of life, and that he had posed for the carving, himself.

What a story, what a great protest. I must have one, but they are too big to carry, he thought. *I will buy a half-size one; it is going to surprise a lot of people and shock a few too.* He was rambling on to himself when a line of saffron-robed monks headed towards him. The leading monk stopped the line, turned to Miles, pointing his finger, then said in an inquisitive way, "You hippie?"

"You monk?" came the quick reply, with the grinning Miles returning the finger. The monk turned and continued on, with each monk wearing a suppressed smile. The serenity of Buddhism was everywhere. It was the whole Thai culture that you breathed in, it was calmness all around you. Miles was a willing student in this global classroom. He loved learning from ordinary country people.

He was following a route that his friend Blinky Tom had told him about. This meant a bus trip to Ban Fang and locating a Mr Chance who would take people trekking up the mountain. The following day he found Mr Chance by chance, soon after stepping off the bus in Fang. He told Miles the trek was starting out the next morning and to buy a flask of Thai whiskey for the chief of the village as a thank-you for allowing them to stay overnight. In the morning, there he was again, the Hat. He called himself Peepol, and Miles began to feel uneasy in his presence. There were five of them who set out on the uphill trek, which turned into a climb late in the afternoon. *Surely there is an easier way to this village*, thought Miles as he kept on climbing until he reached a flat plateau and the native tribe's compound. They were all exhausted as customary greetings were enjoyed and day turned to night.

Mr Chance introduced each member of the group. "This is Mary Anbright, Peepol Tinkwai, My Balls Itch a Lot, Gordon Proper." They all bowed, as they presented the chief with flasks of whiskey and the smiling group were then led to a leafy hut and given rice and something Miles could not work out what it was – he did not want to ask after the dog episode. After they finished, Mr Chance called Miles over to speak with the chief, and with him came Gordon and Mary. Gordon Proper was a Scotsman who was keen to be involved, as was Mary Anbright, an Australian girl from Balmain, in Sydney. Gordon entertained everybody with his harmonica, which delighted the villagers; one lady who was enjoying herself had a huge goitre on her neck, which had Miles wondering how she could get treatment way up here in the mountains. Mary had been telling Miles that the little fella in the hat had not brought any whiskey for the chief. She was cosying up to Miles as if for protection, because she had felt bad vibes from the Hat.

The village chief took great interest in the visitors, and during the evening he became wary of the quiet man in the hat. He called some of the villagers over and said that the Hat would be watched from now on.

It is a beautiful new day. That is how Miles would welcome the morning, always positive. He awoke early, and without disturbing Mary on the floor beside him, he was up, eager to explore and go for a stroll. The air was fresh, pure, delicious to breathe. He drank the water that was channelled to the village through bamboo pipes, so clean that it sang like a good wine. He was locked in the moment; this was the Golden Triangle. He was standing where nature expressed herself to such a divine pinnacle, beauty all around. Peace and joy engulfed him and he could see Burma and Laos, a country he was soon to enjoy.

After a breakfast of rice and that other thing, the group packed up, said their goodbyes and set out on a leisurely descent back down to Fang. The Hat had positioned himself in the rear behind Miles as they set out in single file. He was like a tiger with his prey, but as the Hat was about to strike, he never knew what hit him; Miles turned and looked up to see the smiling chief and some villagers waving goodbye to Miles, who wondered what happened to the Hat, unaware of any drama going on around him. He would not see the Hat again and told Mr Chance he had been left behind.

"Do not worry, Mr Itchy, the chief will look after him", replied Mr Chance. Miles was to catch a bus to Tha Ton the next morning; it was a village not far away from where he could take a boat trip to Chiang Rai.

"Mary", Miles said smoothly to his attractive companion, who was standing just in front of him by the hotel. "Would you like to share the room cost"?

She turned, feigning indignation, saying that she had already paid for her room, then smiled when agreeing to share if he bought dinner. It was a memorable night, and Mary would accompany him the next day on the bus and ferry where they had an affectionate parting on the landing stage.

Chiang Rai was another city of splendour; the architectural beauty of the temples was a fascinating display of their cultural history. Miles had a lust for knowledge, ingesting every moment his route was taking him. He took a bus to Chiang Khong and then a narrow canoe along a fast-flowing river with rapids, occasionally having to get out and carry the canoe before reaching Ban Houei Sai. There was a structure made from corrugated iron that offered scant shade from the hot sun for passengers flying to Luang Prabang in Laos. He looked across the airstrip to see a small passenger plane bring up the dirt on its bumpy landing. *Captain Kangaroo is still alive*, he thought as the plane came to stop close to the shelter.

Not having enough Thai baht left, he paid for a ticket to Vientiane with a mixture of currencies. He used the US dollars he kept in cash for emergencies, as they were always accepted. He was one of a half dozen young travellers waiting to be summoned to a plane. The call came and they all walked over to the door at the side of the aircraft. The first two on board claimed the two seats against the bulkhead. A German was next on board; he sat down, banging his hands on the floor, shouting, "I do not believe it!" The aircraft had been converted to carry cargo and there were no other seats, just rings on the floor to hang on to. Miles laughed to himself at the irate actions of the sour kraut with poor karma, but as Captain Kangaroo was flying the crate, he would wait for the next one.

For two hours, Miles and the other three remaining travellers sat beneath the corrugated shelter. With him were Paddy, Froggy and the Mutt, a now becalmed German, real name, Helmut Koch. He spoke with a strong German accent when he said, "You can call me what you will, but I do not like being called Herr Koch, it could catch on". He was a German student of world history and was researching Thai social history and culture, studying the connection between the people and the king.

"It works; it is harmony", he said. "The Thai people love their unique identity, and it is through the royal family they learn their history. The king does not possess the power he once held but he does hold the love and respect of the people. The king is the head of state, and the royal family give them their own unique identity."

"Isn't that the truth", said Paddy. They spent the time talking together. They all had a common interest, and they were soon good friends. The expected happened as Miles would now be known as Itchy after some bizarre introductions. Paddy, real name Patrick Fields, was an amusing Irishman with a big bushy red beard who spoke a lot about how he was brought up in Galway on the west coast of Ireland.

"Paddy Fields from the bogs of Ireland", came his jovial introduction. "I am here to find the truth about God. When I was a child, I was told what to believe, I had no choice, there was no choice. You could be accused of heresy if you questioned the faith. Fear being used to protect their belief. But when there is doubt, there is a need to find the truth, and when the troubles reappeared back home, I began to doubt my religion a lot, a religion that was built on fear, protected by fear. People lived in fear and died in fear, so different to the wisdom of The Buddha who teaches a different way of thinking."

Paddy continued, that from birth until he left on his mission, he had been told to believe in God, their God, the Catholic God, the true God. He was serious when stating, "I mean, what sort of God creates so much pain and misery for people by throwing in dangerous animals, weather, plants and disease? All over the world people believe in God, their god or gods, for without they are lost souls. People need to believe so they can belong, but here we have a way of life and no God". Paddy wanted to find out more, and he and Miles bonded immediately, both being on the same mission.

Froggy's real name was Iman Amfibian from Moonee Ponds, Melbourne. He was dressed in a Thai sarong and spoke as if he was stoned when he told of how he had been living at a commune in Nimbin, NSW, and was on a quest for the purpose in life.

"We are of the animal kingdom; we are not vegetable or mineral, that is the truth, so we respect all creatures and the earth as we experience survival. That is most common in all creatures and we must not lose connection with the animals. We have to develop an understanding of human nature, but most of all we have a duty to be happy."

"Isn't that the truth", said Paddy.

A grey-haired, stocky man in overalls, holding a can of beer, began to beckon them over to a plane that had been there all along, and that looked more like a shed with wings, but it did have seats.

"Is he the pilot?" asked Mutty, showing great concern.

"That's yeh man alright", said Paddy, equally worried.

The pilot surprised them all with a smooth take-off and a smooth touchdown in Luang Prabang. On the short flight, Miles looked down to see the green tops of the Laos jungle. Only a few years before he had spent twelve months in the Vietnam jungle, not many miles away, and although Australia had pulled out of the conflict, the war was still going on. A weird feeling came over him of suppressed emotion; he had blanked Vietnam out of his mind, as they had been portrayed as villains not heroes by the public on their return from the war zone. He was now a man of peace, but as he looked down, anxieties crept into his mind. It felt surreal. Down below, the Pathet Lao guerrillas were still active, and by the time they landed, he was in defence mode.

It was cost-effective for travellers to share rooms, and it was Miles and Paddy who decided to room together, as they were quick to store their bags and go explore. Miles cashed a $10 travellers' cheque and was handed a fistful of notes; you got a lot of the Kip currency for the dollar.

Luang Prabang was a small town situated in the mountains, with many ornate pagodas. They were strolling along when they were joined by Mutty and the Frog. It was a warm day and they came across boys bathing in a naturally formed pool. They needed no invitation as they gleefully leapt in to freshen up before dinner. There was a Western guy already in the pool who introduced himself as Justin Damood. "But you can call me Scouse", he said. He was the same build as Miles, free-spirited and a lot of fun, being eager to join in. Miles had developed a sore tooth and rice was all he could eat; he told the others he would go see a dentist in Vientiane on the morrow. They had all bought the same ticket with stopover in Luang and decided they would go too.

"I have something that will help", said the Frog, as he brought out a bamboo bong and some Thai stick – that is a smoking device and some strong grass.

"I'm up for that", said Scouse, who easily melted into the company. The desired effect was achieved as Miles slept till morning, only for the ache to reappear.

It was the same plane but different pilot that took them to Vientiane, and after finding a hotel, Miles went searching for a dentist. Buddhism was still very prominent but there was a strong French colonial presence in the city. He saw a shop window displaying a Dentist sign and headed for it. The tooth was aching as he looked through the window and saw a man pedalling a stationary bicycle that worked the dentist drill. *Maybe not*, he quickly decided, so he headed over to the French area where he saw a shop named Phillippe De Cavaire Tea Rooms and Dentistry. *This looks safer*, he thought, so he quickly entered the office, where he was soon attended to.

The offending tooth was drilled and filled much to the relief of the suffering Miles. He went back to find his companions all stoned, with Scouse in the thick of it. The Frog had the bong and passed it to Miles as he came in and sat by the table with marijuana strewn freely across it. An hour went by as they talked about war, with it being in the proximity.

"What are they fighting about?" asked Paddy. "You would think we should have evolved enough not to have to resort to war to solve problems. Religion, that is the reason for the troubles back home, and the many wars through the ages, and where is God? Whose side is he on?"

"I studied Greek philosophy", said Mutty, "and I can still remember what Plato wrote. *'Only the dead have seen the end of war'*, a quote that still rings true today".

"I understand and agree with Paddy", said Miles. "It is big business; like religion is all about selling God. War is all about selling arms and ammunition – without war, no business. Wars are developed all around the world to keep the business going. It is the people who have to fight the wars. I was one, and it is lots of innocent people that get killed and wounded while those that create the conflicts sit back and count the money. Understanding is the way to peace, and these purveyors of grief do not want to listen. Life is cheap to them."

Paddy came in with, "You must have been a bit messed up. How was it?"

"Well, quite frankly, I do not talk about my time in Vietnam. I think it is a self-preservation thing, but at the same time, I loved the army, not so much being shot at but the mateship – every one of my comrades is in my heart." Miles's response was passionate and then he told them he was off in the morning, catching a train to Bangkok, cheaper to keep moving he said.

"Can I join you? I'm heading that way; I want to see more of Bangkok before I have to fly back to the UK", said Scouse.

"No worries, pal, glad of the company", Miles replied. They all sauntered over to a French outdoor cafe. They ate as they talked and exchanged addresses, all the while just taking in the moment, enjoying the surroundings and the companionship.

A young lady was sitting on her own at a table close by and Miles struck up a conversation. "Hi, I'm Miles, but they call me Itchy, and you are welcome to join us if you wish."

"Thank you, but I am a bit weary of you lot, you all look stoned", she said in a defensive voice.

"Because we are", said Miles. "What's your name?"

"Bella, Bella Patra", was the reply.

"I bet they call you Cleo", returned Miles.

"No, I am known as Snow, Snow White", she said in an American accent. "That was my job in Disneyland."

Miles sat down next to her and they chatted and laughed until Paddy came over. "We are going back now", he said.

"Don't worry about me", said Miles. "I'll be with you in five or ten minutes."

"Yeah, sure you will", said Paddy.

Snow White and Miles were getting on extremely well when Paddy left them to it. He had earlier suggested they all make a pact to keep in touch at Christmas. He had said that although it was a Christian and Western celebration, the spirit of Christmas extended to the whole world; it was universal. Plus, they should all have made it home by then and it was a good way to stay connected. The Catholic upbringing he could not shake was still showing through.

A new day of joy to explore was his positive attitude, as in the morning he dressed in his smart shirt and trousers, waving them all goodbye, as he got in a car with Scouse, taking them down to the river. The canoe boat ride down the Mekong had Miles peering nervously into the undergrowth, as they paddled slowly towards the Thai border checkpoint. The smart-looking Miles breezed through the customs and onto a bus to Bangkok, while Scouse went through a more thorough search. They arrived late in the evening but were still able to get food and board at the Honey Pot Hotel. Miles did not want to hang about too long, and he told Scouse he would leave early in the morning for the airport and wait for the next flight going to Calcutta. They had become good friends, and Scouse said they should meet up again when back in England and they exchanged addresses. He was at the airport early in the morning and waited only a couple of hours before catching a plane for Calcutta, West Bengal, India

Chapter Four

---ᴄᴧᴐ---

India

As the plane took off, Miles was regretting being unable to cross overland through Burma and leaving the kingdoms of the Orient, where he had engrossed himself in their culture. The transition into India, from up in the sky, was not what he had hoped for. He had heard a lot about India, and it was exciting him. Calcutta was a name that conjured up intrigue and thoughts of historical events like the Black Hole, and he wanted to embrace their culture.

"Hi, I'm Robin Banks", said the American seated next to him.

"Call me Itchy", he replied, smiling, pre-empting the usual awkward introductions.

Robin was a trainee doctor who was told to take time out, after he questioned aspects of the profession that university authorities objected to. He was interested in alternative medicine and herbal cures, and he had questioned why natural remedies could not be integrated into Western medicine, instead of relying on costly pharmaceuticals. He had pointed out that Chinese natural remedies were still integral to the health system in the Far East. Massage and acupuncture, tiger balm and ginseng, these could all be exploited. He told Miles that he was beginning to believe that doctoring was all about selling pills and making money. Money was becoming more important than the patient, taking advantage of human compassion and of the doctors who truly want to serve the people. He was into the third week of exploring the use of herbal remedies in Eastern practices out of his six-week informal suspension. He went on to say that ginseng was a powerful medicinal root, widely used in the East, but it did not help sell their pills.

"Have you heard of ashwagandha? it is similar to ginseng, and I have to find out more. That is what I will be looking for when we touch down; there is so much benefit from natural remedies, but all the medical schools are sponsored by the big pharmaceutical companies and so promote their products."

They chatted through the whole flight and agreed to go together to the hotel address that Miles produced from his journal. He was ready for anything, or so he thought, as they ventured out of the airport and into the real Calcutta. There was an atmosphere of chaos, friendly but overpowering: homeless children, beggars with their arms outstretched and many people insisting they go with them. They crowded around them. "Namaste", they spoke with hands joined as in prayer; it was enjoyable, with jovial exchanges aplenty, before managing to escape to the Singh Songooley Hotel, both agreeing that their introduction to India was intimidating and crazy. Miles changed immediately into his traveller clothes. Looking the poor hippie, there was lesser chance of being bothered by beggars and was in keeping with cheap lodgings.

He stayed in the Singh Songooley for a few days, ingesting India, its people, its food, *Ah! Its food!* He was sure to be careful here. Robin had left after the first night after not finding the grubby hotel to his liking. He had said, "Send me a card sometime", as he went off searching for the herbal cure. Miles would go walkabouts, and there were always the followers who wanted to be friends and would tag on behind him as he left the Singh Songooley. They would follow him wherever he went; when he stopped, they stopped. He had not gone too far when he stopped in amazement, as before him on the pavement there was a man cutting hair. The barber was keen to cut his now shoulder-length, blond hair as Miles took to the chair. The excited public created a spectacle scrambling to pick up the sun-bleached threads as the barber cut his locks.

"Namaste, namaste", he said, bowing to the barber. He looked to see that there was not a strand of his blond hair to be seen as he went strolling on with his followers in tow.

The wide pavement was a hive of activity, and it was not long before he came across a cobbler. *You can get anything here without stepping off the pavement*, thought Miles as he handed over his well-worn, toe-loop leather sandals. Nothing was wasted here, as a piece of old tyre was cut and shaped for the sandals, which made them heavier but more than capable of getting him home. It was "Namaste, namaste" to the cobbler as he continued to explore, at people level.

He would sit and talk to old, bearded men in the gutter, much to the disapproval of the better dressed public, he had thought they were holy men but found out they were considered untouchables. Still, they would smoke bidis and watch the cars, buses, and the people go by. It was fascinating, like being in a movie. Cows would wander aimlessly through the streets; these sacred beasts were given great respect, only for Miles to ask a Yogi he went on to meet later, "Would they not be better off in a field?" He had met the white- robed Yogi with a beard like a panda by the Dakshineswar Kali temple down by the river. Miles felt comfortable with him; there was a power of knowledge and wisdom emanating through his words. The cow was venerated in Hinduism, and he had smiled at the searching question without answering.

It was his third day in Calcutta when he took a rickshaw ride down to the river to view the temple and *ghats*, when he met the impressive Yogi. Miles was on a spiritual journey and was delighted that the Yogi gave him his time. The *ghats* were steps leading down to the river where people would go to bathe and Miles had asked about the attainment of inner peace.

"You will find that within yourself; first you must trust yourself, trust in that inner feeling. You ask to put old head on young shoulders; first you must travel your own unique path. Once you believe in yourself, you will be more self-confident. It is not easy everyday hearing the noises that are telling you what to do and what to say and how to think. Step back, give yourself a time to meditate, a quiet moment to yourself will enrich your being, and by creating good habits of positive thinking, you will find the

A Cork in a Storm

ability to succeed will come naturally, by focussing on the truth of the moment."

Miles hung on to every word, every movement of this revered man. There was an aura about him; he was in awe of the spirit of peace and wisdom that emanated from this truly holy man. Miles had not been the most patient of people in the past, and this calm exterior was something Miles would like to develop. The next day Miles looked at his map and saw that he had to go north, so the next move would be a train to Benares Varanasi.

Locomotive steam filled the Howrah station amid the accepted mayhem, as Miles fought his way through endless queues to the ticket counter and then the red tape to acquire his sleeper ticket. It was going to be a long journey. The train rolled out of the station amidst the steam, noise and smells, with people crammed into the carriages. He felt like he was still in a movie…it was magic. He would reflect on Calcutta; the wonderful Yogi had inspired him to delve more into this religion. He had bought a book about Hinduism and another book that really delighted him, as he would read about Gandhi. There were quite a few gods here, he was reading, one was not enough. Shiva, Brahma, Vishnu, they seemed to be the main gods, and there were goddesses also. *I should be more educated by the time I reach Benares*, he thought.

The train stopped at many dry and dusty stations along the way, and when pulling into these stations he would hear the cry, "*Coppa chai*" from young boys serving tea in clay pots through the train windows. This was life-giving liquid after hours of dry heat and dust; it was like nectar, costing just a few pi. The steam train also picked up non-paying natives who would climb onto the roofs of the carriages. Night came and the luggage rack became his bed; in the morning, he was pressured into the corner of his bed, to become a piece of luggage himself, by the volume of people cramming into the carriage, the closer they got to Varanasi.

The ancient city was built on the banks of the Ganges. It was the holiest of holy Hindu cities. Miles had heard this from many a traveller and from the informative book he was reading. It was the holiest of places to be in, and respect for their beliefs and culture came naturally to our intrepid Mibald. He had refused the food on offer at stations along the way and was now quite hungry. Food stalls were not difficult to find, and the stall with a sign declaring itself Isnot Hafsobad was where he took a drink of *lassi*, a yoghurt drink he found tasty and nourishing, then some samosas, with *dahl* soup and *chapati*; that seemed the safe way to go. Benares was immediately exciting him with its confining roads that were more like alleyways, congested with people and the odd cow. It was an old city and every corner he turned something would amaze him. A naked man stood wearing a shower cap and dark glasses, holding a bicycle. No one turned an eye…it was fascinating. Miles had to ask about this unusual sight and was informed he was serving a penance and would visit each temple in Benares. Behind a temple to Shiva, a mosque could be seen which caught his attention, not expecting the building in such a holy Hindu city.

His lodgings where of the usual modest nature; he was staying just long enough to drop off his bags and continue the tour of amazement. He ventured down one alleyway leading to the *ghats* by the Ganges. As he got near the river, he could see cremations taking place and turned around so as not to show disrespect. Some pilgrims and devotees would go to Benares to spend their final days and could be seen lying on the ground, waiting to die. There were mats on the ground in the alleyway displaying trinkets and stuff left behind by the departed. On one mat were sets of false teeth, some with the gums bright red from chewing beetle nut – maybe there was a set that could fit someone. He could sense the reverence with which the people held this ancient city with its many temples to Lord Shiva; it was sacred.

He returned to his lodgings above an emporium where the owner would try to entice him in, but without success; he was nevertheless curious and promised to explore the store the next day. He was up early and went for a breakfast of chai, *chapati* and *dahl* soup at Isnot Hafsobad; he had not suffered any ill effects so far. The Yogi in Calcutta had inspired him to seek more wisdom from these holy men and he would wait for the opportunity to arise. He strolled through this ancient city down to the *ghats* that stretched along the banks of Benares Varanasi. It was morning, and there was ritual bathing taking place in the river. He thought, *You have to have a strong faith to go in that water, with all sorts floating in it. You would need to take a bath when you come out.* There was much to take in; he walked slowly back, past the historic buildings. There was wonder all around that would keep him constantly amazed. He would stop for chai and *chapati*, loving every minute being alive. There were many temples, each with their own splendid identity that would intrigue him.

There he is, he said to himself, as his gaze fell upon a white-robed man with a long grey beard, squatting in meditation. He looked at peace and he did not want to disturb him, so he squatted close by in anticipation of speaking to him. After a while, the guru had felt his presence and beckoned him closer.

"You have a high energy, young man. What do you seek?" said the holy man.

"Namaste. Energy, what energy?" said Miles, already struck by the aura that surrounded him.

"We all have unseen energy that fluctuates with our thoughts, it comes from within."

Miles had already ingested the wisdom of self-awareness and was searching for more. *Energy, of course. I feel it all the time but take no notice. I must pay more attention to that gut feeling.*

He said, "Yes, I understand energy. I just seek the truth to understand the world, and more knowledge to survive in it."

The guru stared at Miles and smiled as he replied, "You are like an onion, young man, with layers of energy, each connected to each other – mental, physical, emotional, spiritual. The energy you show is you, right now, at this moment. You are revealing your energy. Being in search of the truth and knowledge is good karma on your journey in time. Keeping your energy in good balance is the secret".

This man was more than he had hoped for; he felt humbled in his presence, but he still asked, "How can you do that? I am sorry, that sounded impertinent. I mean, could you help me find the balance?"

The smiling guru had warmed to Miles when he answered, "Yoga and meditation will help keep your energies connected. Practise, till you feel the energy of the universe. Balance in everything is what we need to succeed, but to achieve global harmony, it may take a long, long time. Not until humanity accepts humility and compassion over selfishness and greed, will that day arrive".

Miles was in awe as he stood up bowing. "Namaste", he said. In respect for this man, he thanked him for his time, as the guru kept smiling, and said, "We may meet again yet, in another life". Miles would dwell on the guru's words. *Reincarnation, we will have to explore that probability.*

The following day, Miles bought a train ticket to Raxaul, near the border with Nepal, his next stop. It was much of the same as his first experience on these fun and exciting Indian steam trains: the smells, the noise and the constant movement of people kept Miles enthralled as he peered through the clouds of steam. The journey was again a long one, but he was a lot wiser. He packed samosas to eat on the way and managed also to claim a window seat; he was not going to miss out on the Chai. Kathmandu was his next destination; the trusty journal had lots of information from his traveller friends, and he was filled with excitement about exploring the magic-filled capital of Nepal.

Chapter Five

—⚡—

Nepal

The train pulled into Raxaul the next morning, and as they would not allow you to cross the border on foot; for two rupees, he was able to cross the border to Birganj in Nepal on the back of a horse and cart. He was beginning to feel unwell as he was securing a lift on a truck to Kathmandu, and for ten rupees a deal was done. The truck was very colourful, with a deep storage box above the driver's cab painted in vibrant yellows, oranges and reds; the box was to be his carriage. *This is the Himalayas*, he was thinking, as he climbed up and into the box. *Everest is over there.* The road hugged the mountainside as Miles looked down over such exhilarating beauty from his dangerous but spectacular vantage point. The thrill of it all was being compromised by feeling unwell and he wondered why.

It took about six hours before the truck pulled up beside a large shrine in the heart of Kathmandu, as night began to fall. It had been a fantastic journey perched above the driver's cab looking out over divine natural beauty; it had been breathtaking, but it had taken its toll. Miles was feeling ill like he did in Penang – that was worrying. He needed to find lodgings quickly. The directions he had were easy to follow and was soon being shown a room where he collapsed on his bed exhausted. He awoke the next day feeling much better and after a trip to the toilet, even better again. It must have been the oil in the samosas. *I should be avoiding that*, he thought, as he went a short way to the pie shop. He climbed the stairs up to a balcony leading to a room with a distinct smell of cannabis. It was, as he had been told, a haven for grubby, wonderfully weird hippies, who greeted Miles with, "Come in! You have got to taste the pies, they are great!"

"Hi, they call me Boots."

"Hi, Mibald is my name, but I know you are going to call me Itchy", he replied.

There were four others in the company around a big oblong table that took up most of the room. He sat down and Boots passed him a plate with a slice of apricot pie. "Thank you", said Miles. "Why do they call you Boots?"

"Well, my name is Wellington Hill, and I was a student of American History in the Pioneering West of Nineteenth Century America. I was researching what records I could find about the occupants of Boot Hill, and it wasn't long before a fellow student saw the connection, and called me Boot Hill, which was shortened to Boots", he replied. "Then one day I decided to see more of living than the dead, so here I am. Now, my roommate left yesterday, and would you like to share? It only means moving a few doors down to a twin room and it's half the cost."

"Glad to", was the quick response.

"Shall we smoke on it?" he said, as a large, carrot-shaped joint was handed over by the tall guy with blond dreadlocks, who introduced himself as Hans Ormballs from Sweden.

"Starting the day like this prepares you for the joy the day brings", he said in his Scandinavian accent.

The talk was friendly and free, and they gave each other nicknames as they introduced themselves. "I think we will call Hans, Rasta. Great hair", said Ivor Plumshort from New Zealand. He was the guy with the droopy moustache who they called Chilly, after his favourite smoking device, the chillum. He had bought the marble, cone-shaped pipe at the emporium below the pie shop. Then there was the long-haired Aussie, Bat Anball, who was known as Cricket. He came from Queensland and was learning about the unique Tibetan flute music. There was Bollic Shmeller from Switzerland, an intellectual-looking fellow with glasses, who would later be called Gilly – anything was better than Bollic. He was heading east, from where Miles had just been; they would soon be exchanging notes.

A young Nepalese boy about fourteen had been hovering around and serving pies all the time they were talking; he was in charge and a very amusing character he was. "You just arrive, I look after you, I look after everybody. I Freddy, you need anything, I get. I call you Garuda, you big nose." Everybody laughed and laughed again when "My Balls Itch a Lot" began to explain his name. They were stoned, as Miles – now Garuda – and Boots donned their shades, followed by Bollic, and ventured out. Miles knew that Garuda was a God with an eagle's beak in the Hindu culture. He never thought of his nose being that big before, but being called Garuda was novel.

They wandered through the maze-like alleyways and into the market, where a side of meat was hanging covered with flies, the sight convincing him to stay vegetarian. Boots was leading them to a shop with a sign which read:

SHIVA HASHISH & GANJA CENTRE

Where Friendly People Gather

Best Hashish & Ganja Available Here

GOVT. REG'D.

This was a sign to behold. "Look", said Bollic, "we are friendly people. We have got to get some free samples", spoken in that continental English way. They went upstairs to the first floor of this old building to find the inviting smell of ganja in the form of salami sausages hanging from a display rack.

A sign above the counter read:

Available as always Different Varieties:

WHOLESALER & RETAILER

1. HASHISH (Mustang)
2. HASHISH (Barjang)
3. ATTAR (Hashish)
4. HASHISH JUMLA
5. Tarai Flower Tops
6. Green Ganja
7. Alibam Gana
8. HASHISH OIL

We Are Always At Your Service

The sight of legal cannabis on display, in quantity and quality, was like walking into Aladdin's cave, the smell adding to the magic. They were spoilt for choice but eventually decided on a compressed sausage of green ganja. They were told the shop was having to close as the law had changed and it would no longer be legal to operate.

"Are these the closing down sale prices?" asked Bollic cheekily. "I would like some oil."

The smiling owner placed a vial of hashish oil on the counter. "Here, you take, you poor hippie. Namaste."

"Namaste", echoed the smiling friends as they reversed out of the door, bowing as they went. "That was a bit insensitive", said Boots to Bollic. "He's just lost his business".

"Do not ask, do not get", came the reply.

Haunting flute music met them as they arrived back at the pie shop. Freddy was beckoning them over pointing at the new arrivals, a young Scotsman who introduced himself as Colin Dare and his girlfriend, Jan Hitter. Colin was tall, brash, loud, and very funny, while his girlfriend was small and apologetic. It was unusual to see a female traveller this far up the trail and she was a welcome addition, as they immediately blended in, demolishing the last piece of fruit pie before building a commendable reefer. The group had bonded with ease and when Cricket asked, "Who believes in God?" there was an excited response, as Bollic passed the chillum to the man who had just injected a question that caught everybody's attention.

He took a draw before he continued. "Did God create the universe? If so whose God? If he did, what was he doing for the billions of years before the creation. Why create man at all?"

"That was a lot of questions", said Miles, "but I can tell you I gave up on religion to find the truth about God, and the truth is, God did not create man, man created God. That is all the gods: the Hindu, Jewish, Islamic, Pagan, and the Christian God, who saved the world and the Bible bashers who converted the pagans into Christianity".

It was beginning to get serious, when a profound Rasta said, "We can only find truth when there is no prejudice. One must keep an open mind; the truth has no branches in the tree of life".

"Are you a Christian" said Cricket to Colin, who was struggling with the end of a joint, Heck no, thank God I'm an atheist. Then he came in with, "It depends on where you are born as to which god you believe in".

"That is true, but what is important to remember is that the child is innocent; it is the parents who instill whatever belief they have onto their young", said Cricket.

"Who wrote the Bible?" Jan exclaimed out of nowhere, eager to be involved. "And for that matter, who wrote the Quran, the Muslim version of salvation?"

There was a pause as Freddy brought in a fresh pie and placed it on the table. The chillum was passed around, and Colin provided a splendid reefer to get sparked up. Miles had been deep in thought before he said, "People need something to believe in and these texts of moral guidance would have been easy to accept for the people of the time. 'God's law', what could be better?" Stated Miles, "Gods were created by man for something to believe in; they had to. Let's face it, Moses, what a great story, but who dreamed it up? The early civilizations, like Mesopotamia, would have believed in something, but it was not Christianity or Islam; they had not been invented. Man brought in laws and invented holy scriptures – the Bible, the Quran – with wonderful stories of good against evil, moral codes for people to believe in. They had to believe in something and still do. Like Santa Claus, we are taught to believe in something unbelievable early in life. It takes strength to accept the truth, especially when being challenged by a belief. People will only believe what they want to, even when it is not the truth".

"Yeah", said Boots. "People will only read what they want to believe, whether it be true or not, but they do have to believe in something."

Miles came back again. "Well, of course, *'the eyes will see only what the mind wants to hear'*. Belonging, that is the most principal factor in human survival, safety in numbers. A person with faith will enjoy life in a way we cannot; we are all doomed if we do not believe in God."

"The problem I have with people of faith is they want to convert you into their own belief, strength in numbers", said Boots.

"Darwin's theory of evolution challenged all beliefs and seems the logical way to go", chipped in Cricket.

"It is good that there are more questions than answers coming out here", said Chilly, "and I would like to know, what did they all believe thousands of years ago, in ancient civilisations, before we were all saved?"

"Why do you want to know if there is a God? Does it matter? They say ignorance is bliss", Jan was keen to add.

"Curiosity has driven mankind through the ages", said Bollic, "and I can tell you about ancient civilisations that had such advanced technical and engineering knowledge that it still mystifies man today. The Pyramids, for instance, how were they built? And even before that, all over the world there are structures that man cannot explain. In Puma Punku, on a high plateau in Bolivia, there are gigantic, polished stones with intricate carving. There has been no explanation as to how this was achieved with the tools they would have had. Each of these stones weighing over a hundred tons, how did they move them onto this high plateau from the quarries many miles away? There have been hundreds of lost civilisations in the world. The Aztecs who lived in what is now Mexico, had engineering skills far beyond the imagination, with an understanding of astronomy, the basis of their beliefs. They constructed temples to align with the stars, pointing to the heavens or a spaceship. Many believe these stones could not have been carved by humans, and so maybe God is an alien and comes down in his spaceship every so often to see how we are getting on".

Boots fired in a beauty with, "What if we are descended from aliens? What if God is an alien? Maybe Adam and Eve were aliens; that could be where the story came from. In New Mexico, in 1947, there was reported to have been a crash by a flying saucer. After clearing the crash site, it was quickly hushed up by the government and is still being kept quiet. Then in the early sixties, a couple called Betty and Barney Hill, no relation, I may add, got kidnapped by aliens. It was all over the news, and it has not been disproved. Everything through time points to the stars; this cannot be ignored".

That threw everybody. Aliens, why not? That could explain a lot; they had not touched on that before. The talk was active and would go from one to another. "Will my brains fall out of my open mind?" said Chilly.

The immediate laughter was interrupted with, "Only if you keep your mouth open". This comment by Cricket had everyone in convulsions, and after the jollyferkating had died down, Cricket said, "We are like people searching for truth, a council. I propose we convene as the People's World Council". This was greeted with laughs of approval and a refilling of the chillum. "May I add, this will have no consequence on the world, only us. The truth must be identified and accepted even when it hurts, and it does hurt", said Cricket.

"That is not as easy as it sounds", said Miles. "I would find it hard to tell my folks I do not believe in God. That would hurt them. Sometimes, withholding the truth till the right moment can prevent hurt. Christmas, for instance, we love this untruth for the joy it brings. We identify truth with being good, but it does often bring hurt."

Miles had been happy with his contributions and added, "You know, my sergeant in the army was a Buffalo. He said it was like the Masons, but not quite the same. Religion is not even discussed; the idea is they all look after each other, and like in religion and all societies, the safety is in numbers".

"They have loads of societies and secret lodges in the US", said Boots. "They run the country."

"Islamic countries all believe in the same god. There is no opposition to Mohammad, which makes them strong. We must be careful; they are a powerful religion", said Bollic. "That might be where the next war breaks out."

They carried on until they were too stoned to continue. In the morning it was the same again: a large carrot would be sparked up, pies would be devoured, and they would discuss what to do. Bollic had suggested hiring bikes, when Cricket said to him, "Can we call you something else?"

"Like Smelly?" butted in Chilly.

"Well, that is not much better. What did you work as, Bollic?"

"I am a professor at the Gillam Font of Knowledge Academy in Bern. We are all known as Gillies."

"Sounds a lot better. Gilly, it is. That explains how you know so much about ancient history. What was your subject?" asked Boots.

"Anthropology, Ancient Greek History and Philosophy, which is what I involve myself in most. Aristotle, Socrates, and Plato were great philosophers in their civilisation, the basis for our civilisation today. Their quotes are as true today as they were back then. In our quest for the truth, there are also consequences. My favourite was Plato, and he wrote, *'Those who can see beyond the shadows and lies of their culture will never be understood, let alone believed, by the masses'*. Whatever we accomplish here will never be believed, because we challenge the status quo, and nobody likes change, even when it is for the good. I can tell you more about the many lost civilisations, but what it tells me is that we are just passengers in time. For thousands of years people have come and gone and now it is our turn to help evolution on its way."

Everybody was happy with his new name, and it was Gilly, Miles and Boots who went exploring on bikes, while Cricket, Chilly and Rasta would just float around town. Boots was stoned and nearly fell off his bike as they pedalled out to where they could see Mount Everest. They stopped often at temples and shrines with prayer wheels. The canister-shaped wheels were inscribed with prayers and set into the side of the shrine; when walking around the shrine, you would spin the wheels to say a thousand prayers. They would sit by the shrine and discuss the Tibetan religion; it was just as fascinating as Hinduism, with both having similarities to Buddhism. They decided that religions had variant forms all over the world and it was about what you wanted to believe, and that religion was a superstition, the opium of the people.

There was disappointment when the cloudy skies would not allow them to see Everest, and so began the slow, funny and smoky way home.

They had stopped for a smoke when Miles told of his meeting with a guru in Benares who told him they might meet again in another life.

"Reincarnation is a difficult one to believe", said Gilly, "but not one to dismiss. I am not sure I would want to come back. It's interesting, though".

They went through days in a daze having enormous fun, with Chilly and his chillum starting the proceedings. Boots would make joints for when they were on the road later, while Miles had mastered the art of the seven-skin carrot. One day they had stopped for food near the main square and Miles had an urgent call to visit the toilet. He was in a hurry when he entered the cubicle – such was his haste that his passport pouch slid off his belt and under the door. All he could do was hope, as he could not move, but his hopes were dashed when he opened the door to find it gone. An opportunist had snaffled it up.

He went back to the others and told them of his trouble. "I think I will have to skip breakfast in the morning and find the embassy", he said.

Back at the pie shop, streetwise Freddy was an immense help with the embassy address, American Express office address, and the contact for a new student discount card. He had kept the US dollars in cash separate from his passport and other travel documents for such an emergency; this would see him through until he had everything sorted. During this waiting period, they would talk a lot about Tibetan culture, the Dalai Lama, Buddhism, Hinduism, and why the Western world needed to embrace compassion in their decision making.

"Well, they cannot. It is a capitalist world; everybody wants to make money. No room for compassion", said Chilly during a smoke-filled meeting of the PWC.

"Money makes the world go round. The rich get richer, and the poor get poorer. That is the way it has been and still is", said Boots.

"Where there is much money, there is much corruption", the eager Jan would contribute.

Rasta came in with, "The more money you make, the better you survive, and survival is what life is".

Miles elaborated, "Everybody, the world over, survives somehow in their own way. That is what we creatures of the earth do, survive".

Then there was the day cannabis became illegal. The PWC gathered around the table and each gave a patriotic speech while representing their country on such a unique occasion. Chilly was first to stand and spoke in grave tones. "I represent all free-thinking Kiwis, and raise this chillum bowl to the day when the truth about its medical qualities allows marijuana to be legalised again." He raised the chillum, took a deep draw, passed it to Boots and sat down as the atmosphere became solemn.

"Today is the day for the USA", Boots said rising slowly, "and the money god they adore. I suspect there has been an influence from the US to bring about today's act against the people."

After drawing on the pipe he passed it next to Gilly, who sang, "Money, money, money is surely the reason behind this decision, and more than one country has had an input. On behalf of the Swiss nation, I condemn this outrage against the people. The professor has spoken". He took his smoke and left the chillum on the table next to Rasta, who began to refill the bowl.

Cardboard Col, as he was now called, stood up and fell down again. Rasta stood up saying, "I will speak for Sweden, when I say that other forces are also at work, like Carlsberg, and all the other beer, wine and spirit merchants. They would lose money". He had spoken with purpose. Even as he drew on the pipe, it was with purpose; as he passed the chillum to Cricket, it was with purpose.

Before Cricket could stand up, Cardboard interrupted. He stood up again, despite the efforts of an embarrassed Jan to restrain him, and blurted, "On behalf of the Scottish people, who I don't think give a shit —that is the truth – but I think all governments should legalise all drugs, not ban them. Stands to reason…control of quality, medical information, less crime, and all governments like anything that incurs taxation. This is still a diabolical decision". He took the chillum from Cricket, inhaled deeply and gave it back before he turned onto the balcony and vomited into the street below.

"Crikey, you lot are looking for someone to blame, when we should just accept it. Life changes all the time; this we must understand."

"Isn't that the truth", interrupted Rasta.

"Let us enjoy the moment, my friends. I am happy and proud to represent Australia with you lot of lunatics on such an occasion as this." Cricket was smiling all the time he was speaking; he took a draw and was still smiling when Miles took the pipe from him and began to refill it.

"Bravo, Cricket, that was well said, but now, on behalf of Her Majesty Queen Elizabeth, whom I think may not approve, nevertheless, I applaud everybody's search for the truth, and the truth is, we must accept it. As Cricket says, the real truth is that this is the last day. Not that that means anything, so here is to the truth and our acceptance of it."

Miles sparked the chillum, and everyone was smiling again when from behind the counter came, "I listen you. Me proud to be here too". Freddy continued, "I want to speak for Nepalese people, yes? And I make ganja pie".

Whoops of joy abounded. Cricket whistled on his flute as Freddy brought out the pie. They all ate a slice, apart from the collapsed Colin whom the tormented Jan would eventually revive and bring the night's events to a close.

It was 1st August when Miles was issued a new passport. He already had the replacement traveller's cheques and Freddy had sorted the student card. He had also shown Miles the family emporium below the pie shop with its array of unique Tibetan handicrafts on display, and Freddy wanted to begin an export business. Miles was taken in by his enthusiasm, so he gave him his home address and promised to stay in touch. It had taken some time to get his documents in order, and only Cricket remained as the others had moved on. Now it was his turn. He was going to miss the evening sessions of fun and philosophy, finding truth, understanding what the truth was and how to identify it. They had concluded that they were worse off than people with faith, and that they knew nothing; this was the truth they all agreed upon.

Hugo Furst, a mountaineer from Austria, had just come in from Pokhara where he had been trekking and showed Miles the road he had to take. Freddy gave him a big hug and a price list and Miles waved goodbye as he strode out of town going west. He was now carrying two bags, as he had purchased a Hessian bag off Freddy, with a colourful Tibetan shoulder strap. He walked at a leisurely pace holding out his thumb, but no one stopped. He had been walking for hours, and the night was drawing in when from a small house dwelling across the road, a man beckoned him over. The man could see Miles was stranded and invited him in, where they made him feel welcome. They fed him and gave shelter for the night.

A traveller in need was cared for by these compassionate Nepalese country people.

In the morning it was "Namaste". His hosts had arranged a lift for him on the back of a truck to Pokhara. He was so grateful to them as he climbed up onto the truck waving goodbye, unable to thank them as he would have liked. What wonderful people. He was a stranger, a foreigner, and yet they could not do enough to help. He had paid the driver ten rupees for the lift, which he gladly agreed to after his efforts of hitching the day before. He felt privileged travelling on the back of a truck breathing in the clean, fresh air and gazing on the mountains, feeling connected with the earth. Pokhara had its own splendour with the backdrop of snow-covered mountains, but he literally had to put them behind him. With the mountains at his back, he took a long bus ride out of Nepal, to Nautanwa.

Chapter Six

Middle East

He had crossed the border back into India, and the train station was at Gorakhpur. A five-rupee taxi ride took him there. He climbed aboard a train back to Benares and got himself as comfortable as possible, knowing what to expect. He took out his map and cried to himself, "Crikey, what am I doing? I am going the wrong way!" Money was now dangerously low; having the extra expense of taking more trains was irritating him until the train slowed down and he heard the cry, "*Coppa chai*". He was hoping to take the train to Agra without having to stay overnight in Benares, but that did not happen. The train to Agra was leaving the following day, so he went back to his old lodgings to be greeted by Gobsheet, who was happy to see him again.

The rooms were above the Brocade Emporium run by Gobsheet, who was a Muslim in a holy Hindu city. He had been trying to set up an export business with Miles on his first visit and now Miles was getting interested. He had not been into the emporium as he had promised on his first visit, and Gobsheet gave him a list of what the emporium sold. Silk and gold scarves, sitars, ornate chess sets, ivory anything, water pipes, chillums of many varieties: plain marble, carved marble, and carved wooden chillums of rosewood, teak, sandalwood and ebony. One ornately carved sandalwood chillum with a marble bowl took his eye. It was cheap enough and he would be able to sell it when he got home. This could be the start of an export enterprise, as he had Freddy in Nepal as a contact and now Gobsheet in Benares.

With price lists and bank details in place, he put the chillum in his bag and went walkabouts. There was a holy man squatting outside a temple to Shiva, the same temple but different guru that Miles had met on his first visit. Could it happen again? He strolled by, eagerly wishing to speak to him, when the man smiled in a beckoning fashion, so he went over and sat on his haunches beside him.

"Namaste." They talked for a long time about life in India; he was truly a wise guru. He spoke of the need to find balance in everything: too much was as bad as too little. Miles was impressed by the way the conversation had gone. He talked to the guru about the people he had met since starting the journey, some searching for true happiness, inner peace and enlightenment; others, the meaning of life or the purpose of life.

"Search no more", the guru said, as Miles's eyes lit up. *Is this it?* he thought. *Am I going to feel the wisdom?*

"There is no meaning to life. It is both meaningful and meaningless; it is what you make it. There is no purpose in life; life is you, now, this moment", said the guru. "Do not be distracted by future desires; focus on the moment and you will be rewarded. Happiness is found within; look inside yourself for peace and joy, not outside."

It had been an enlightening encounter, with the guru concluding, "You jolly man, you live till eighty-six". *That is nice to know*, he thought.

"Namaste." He bowed and went to the Isnot Hafsobad food stall for some *dahl* soup and *chapatis* while he pondered over his meeting with the guru. Buddhism taught mindfulness and to focus on the moment, much in the same way as Hinduism; this was constant. *That is what life is.* He reflected on what Ghandi had written:

> **"In the midst of death, life persists. In the midst of untruth, truth persists. In the midst of darkness, light persists. Hence, I gather that God is Life, Truth and Love."**

He used the morning to wander the ancient city taking in every moment, as he slowly made his way to the station to take the train to Agra. While on the journey, he once again consulted his journal. One of his traveller friends had sketched a diagram of where to stay; it was quite detailed, and it showed the Red Fort by the river and arrows pointing to an X with the name Mr Goan Chunda. He had a restaurant and would put up travellers at the back for a few rupees. It was easy to find and on the way there, he took in the moment when he gazed in wonder at the Taj Mahal. His eyes hurt from the glare off the white marble in the bright sunshine. At night, the moon changed its lustre to a shimmering pale blue, a glorious sight against a clear sky, and yet it looked insignificant against the star-filled universe.

He was moving on the next day, and that was confirmed after he found his bed to have a colony of fleas, forcing him to sleep on the floor. He took a bus to New Delhi the next day after first beating his camouflaged ex-army poncho liner he used as a blanket; it was lightweight, warm and now full of fleas. Two more travel visas were needed for Afghanistan and Iran and, fortunately, the embassies were close together, so he did not lose too much time. He did not want to stay too long, for after paying for the visas he would only have fifty US dollars left.

He had a sleeper inclusive train ticket to Amritsar that he had bought earlier; he was reluctant to leave, as he loved India and wanted to stay, but he had to keep moving. He had seen Westerners begging on the streets of New Delhi and knew he could not afford to stop. He had picked up a book to read on the train, written by Bhagwan Shree Rajneesh, called *The Inward Revolution*. He was wanting to increase his understanding of Indian culture. There was a lot to take in, but he found it enjoyable and so easy to absorb. He was reading what he wanted to hear; this was a truly wise man.

Amritsar in the Punjab was different territory. He could feel it when he stepped off the train; he could sense the change. The Sikh Golden Temple could be seen from the bus stop, a sacred temple in Sikhism, but he had no time to linger as the bus was leaving shortly for Lahore. It was a small bus with a big Sikh as the driver. There were just six passengers, all Westerners, and Miles got chatting to a French guy, Jacques De Ripaire, a typical unkempt traveller. He was heading back to Paris after spending time roaming India, searching for inner peace.

They had not travelled too far when a young Sikh boy made an accusation that someone had not paid. This was not true. He was irritating and loud, and Jacques grabbed him by the shirt, hoisting him in the air and telling the boy everybody had paid and to stop being a little shit. The bus stopped and the driver came from behind the wheel in a menacing manner. "Jacques, put him down", cried Miles, as a huge Swedish guy stood up, giving the driver a stern look, and it all calmed down. *Jacques has not found his peace*, thought Miles. Still, they had agreed to share costs along the way.

They crossed the border into the walled city of Lahore without further incident. Mosques were now to be seen as they had also crossed into an Islamic state. The next day they took a bus to Peshawar in Western Pakistan; there were no more temples, as Mosques would now be the houses of worship for the people. How distinctive the change was in just a few days overland. It had become a race against his money running out; he had to keep moving.

The bus trip across Pakistan saw the landscape becoming even more dry as the road took them due west. After a night in Peshawar, they bought bus tickets to Kabul, which meant the bus had to stop as they went through a customs checkpoint at the Khyber Pass. Miles was having a moment, looking up at the walls of the Pass, envisioning the snipers up in the rocks during the conflicts that took place there many times through the ages, when he heard a ruckus going on in the shed.

"Jacques, put him down", cried Miles. "Put him down!" The customs man was being held over the counter by Jacques; he was confiscating a volume of Karl Marx and Jacques was reluctant to let go of it, or the official. Miles managed to pacify all involved until he became annoyed himself when they took his "Man in a Barrel." *That was not fair… I could have had some fun with that,* thought a disgruntled Miles. *Well, the parcel is still safe, anyway.*

The journey to Kabul was long and uneventful but after finding a hotel with a group of travellers, the day turned to eventful. Most of them were heading for India and had been smoking hashish from a hookah pipe when Miles and Jacques joined them. Soon the party started. They had all convened to the room of the new arrivals, bringing the hookah with them.

There were five of them travelling east and they were eager to learn about India and beyond, while Miles was keen on finding cheap places to stay on the western trail. Jacques was a talented linguist and was the interpreter as they all enjoyed this impromptu international party. As travellers do, they all shared rooms. There was Abass Teedo with Amla Fing from Amsterdam, on their way to Kathmandu. Igor Depetcat and Ivan Dalise were heading for Goa and came from Finland. Ty Curry, from New York, was also heading for Goa, which was becoming a hippie haven. He shared with the German, Gude Farht, who was heading west.

Smoke filled the room as the hotel manager walked in with the police, and everybody froze. There was still a warm chillum, a smoking hookah, and hashish strewn across the low table. The policeman said something sternly in Afghani, while the manager told the company to keep the noise down and walked back out. Nobody had moved.

"Have we just been busted?" Miles said in disbelief. "Busted in Kabul. Hey, that could be a good line for a song." Everybody laughed and continued to exchange notes and tell stories. Gude Farht, the German who had escaped to India after being accused of joining the Red Army Faction, RAF, a left-wing terror group, was now in a similar state of finance as Miles and would be on the same bus to Herat in the morning.

Sitting outside in the sunshine having breakfast, Jacques was telling Miles that they could meet up again in Istanbul as he already had a ticket to fly out the following week. He was drawing a sketch of where to meet, when a young boy waiter came over demanding more money. The boy was instantly thrust into the air.

"Jacques, put him down", was again the cry from Miles, thinking this was becoming a habit, as he again pacified the dispute.

Waving goodbye to all, Miles joined Gude on the bus for the long journey through the barren landscape to Herat, an oasis town with ancient history, and now he had another companion to share the road with. Miles had an insatiable lust for learning and was eager to explore the historic Citadel. On finding their lodgings, they ventured out into the town. Miles was wearing shorts and quickly returned to the hotel to change into trousers, as he was getting heckled by young boys pointing at his legs. He realised nobody else had their legs exposed and it must be forbidden to show a bit of leg. You could only see the eyes of the women. *This Islam is so restricting*, he thought, *and has to be male orientated*.

After a night in Herat, they took a minibus to Taybad in Iran and then it was onto a bus to Meshed; a train would take them to Tehran. On the train he was talking to Amir Phoralaf, a student from Mashed studying in Tehran; he was telling him about how the people were not happy with the Shah flaunting his wealth while much poverty still existed.

"It is the same the world over", said Miles, "the rich exploiting the poor. Always has been. One day the meek shall inherit the earth". He looked at his map and Iran looked large, even on his map, and Turkey the next country to traverse, even bigger. They were going the right way, at least, and once in Tehran, they were to take a bus to Bazergan. Gude was good company, and they talked long about the Red Army and why he fled to escape it and the Politz. He had been in the company of some of its members who were trying to recruit him when they got raided and everybody ran. He said India seemed a good place to get lost in, but one must face up to adversity and he was going to prove he had not been involved.

"I know it is not the same, but I did my National Service", said Miles, "and even thought about signing on again. I enjoyed it, made many friends who will be in my heart for life. That Red Army, though, is not quite the same".

They slept in the bus shelter from where they would take a minibus to a village on the border. Once on the bus, they passed through the customs, which was no more than a shed, and into Turkey. They sat in the large square under the early morning sun, drinking coffee, which was short, strong and black. The men of the village were also sitting around with their coffee; there were no children or women, until a troop of women carrying farm tools appeared as they were escorted through the village. "What an extraordinary sight", said Miles then sang, "Hey, Gude…what do you make of that? And look at that mountain over there – it will be Mount Ararat. That is where the Bible says the Ark landed after the great flood".

Gude said, "We better get moving. Let us ask that man by the truck". There was more than a hint of unease in his voice. He had diverted the talk away from Mount Ararat; he wanted to leave. A deal was done for fifteen Turkish lire each, to take them to Erzurum, and as the truck began to pull out of the village, young boys appeared and threw stones at the two exposed travellers on the back.

"They do not make you feel welcome", said Gude, the stone-throwing supporting his first impression.

The road to Istanbul, via Ankara, was eventful in many ways, as they would travel mostly on the back of open trucks. They had to pay the drivers but would sleep on the trucks that carried them and noticed it was getting colder the farther west they went. One morning, when the cold was so intense the chill had reached the marrow, they banged on the cab of the open-backed truck, trying to get him to stop; they had not known cold like this, ever. However, the driver kept going till he had reached where he was going. The usual thank-yous were dispensed with as Gude began to run down the road to get some feeling back. Miles never expected Turkey could be so cold, and to get warm, he started to do the exercises remembered from his days in the army. They walked for long ways, and on one night as the cold was setting in, they walked onto a building site were the night watchman allowed them to bed down next to the fire he kept ablaze in the drum. He made them coffee in the morning, and they thanked him heartily, as it was lifesaving warmth he had given these travellers in need. As they walked along, Miles would sing, "Keep right on to the end of the road, keep right on till the end", then after a while, Gude began to join in much to Miles's amusement, and they laughed as he encouraged him along the road.

In Ankara, they got a lift from an off-duty taxi to the edge of the city, pointing them in the right direction for Istanbul. To their surprise the driver passed a joint over to them in the back, which they were happy to share, even though Miles had given up smoking that very morning after a spate of coughing and gave his cigarettes to Gude, vowing never to smoke again. He then turned to Gude saying, "I said nothing about hashish". They had reached Istanbul, a city divided in two by the Bosphorus Strait and were trying to find enough money for the ferry. Squatting by the river, they looked at the assorted currencies they had between them and laid it all out on the ground. A kind man standing near could see the dilemma and made up the shortfall for them to have enough money to cross the river and into Europe. Miles looked at the sketch in his journal that Jacques had drawn, and the pudding shop was the meeting place near the Blue

Mosque. As they got close, a ruckus could be heard. *Oh no,* thought Miles, as he entered the shop and cried, "Jacques, put him down!" Once again, Jacques had hold of the unfortunate employee who had tried to charge him for leaving a note for Miles on the notice board. The clamour soon died down and they enjoyed short, strong black coffee, as Gude told them he was going to keep moving.

"I will send you a card", said Miles, as they embraced and shook hands.

"I may be in the jail", Gude Farht groaned, and Miles began to sing after him, "Keep right on to the end of the road". Gude laughed as he waved goodbye. The two friends went back to the cheap hotel that Jacques had found so Miles could drop off his bags. They were going for a Turkish bath. These historic stone-built caverns were stunning; he was envisioning them being used centuries ago. Pockets of steam could be seen rising from areas where large loin-clad men with mop heads in their hands were scrubbing the backs of customers in this wonderful ancient environment. It was an expense he could not afford but an opportunity he could not miss. After a good rub down, he had never felt so clean; he was tingling as he felt privileged just being in such a fabulous place.

They spent the night in Istanbul, taking in what they could, and then it was time to move on. "Ring me when you get to Paris", said Jacques as Miles climbed onto a bus to take him to the outskirts of the city.

"I may need to", said Miles, smiling.

Chapter Seven

Europe

It was hitchhiking and more sleeping rough from here on as it took two days to pass through Greece. Miles walked out of Turkey and into the Greek town of Alexandroupolis. Not having much luck with getting a lift, he was quick to jump on the back of a slowed-down truck which took him to Kavala. An imposing fortress looked down over the city as night began to fall, and Miles went looking for food and somewhere to sleep. He was now permanently hungry and found he could afford the local bread, which would only sustain him till morning and the hunger would start again. He had slept well under a secluded bush near the shore of the Aegean Sea, and apart from the hunger he felt quite good. He picked up more bread and hitched a ride, once again, on the back of a truck that took him to Thessaloniki, a great city full of ancient history, in which a frustrated Miles had no time to explore. There was so much to take in, but his priority was to find a camp spot. Down to the beach was always a safe way to go, and so it was, with plenty of space available.

He sat down in a quiet section of the beach and began to eat some bread and olives, when two young local girls stood and stared at him. A pronounced "How are you?" came from the extremely attractive one of the two who had been articulate with her English. "My name is Demeter and this my friend Aphrodite. Where have you been and where are you going?"

Miles was immediately attracted to the dark-eyed beauty with short black hair and was glad to answer anything a Grecian goddess like her should ask. Demeter, also, showed a keen interest in this man of the road and sat down beside him; she was curious to learn of his travels and himself in particular. They chatted freely; she had never met anybody so interesting before and when she realised, he had no money, she offered to buy him dinner in the nearby cafe. Her friend had left them together and the food was gratefully accepted as was the company, for she was not only gifted with flawless beauty, but she was fun and had a yearning for knowledge of the world outside the confines of her community.

They talked for hours not realising the time passing, both enjoying each other's company. they talked of ancient Greece and the great philosophers, and she was surprised by the interest that Miles showed. She, however, was interested in Miles and where he was going, so they strolled back down to the beach to continue their evening together. She read out, "My Balls Itch a Lot", from his passport that he showed her as she was so curious, but she knew this would be just a passing encounter. They nestled down by the sea so they could finish the wine and take their time to say goodbye. She had written her name, Demeter Nickordropolis, in his journal and he promised to write when he got home.

In the morning, he was reflecting on his good fortune; she had lifted his resolve to succeed, and he would certainly be keeping in touch with her. He freshened up in the sea before he ploughed on and into Yugoslavia, when luck shined brightly on him as he was picked up by a honeymooning couple. Tobias Thyme and his new wife Hextra were a French couple from Auxerre, who had been to Athens and were touring their way to Hungary before going home. The comfort of a car ride was a welcome change as they drove to Skopje then onto Beograd and Zagreb. That took two days and all the way across in one lift. He would sleep in the car when they had a hotel stop, and they bought food in the markets and picnic along the way. They were good, kind and inquisitive people who loved the stories Miles would tell and were eager to learn of how religions changed and differed from the Far East to Europe.

Over the days they were together, Miles would tell of the compassion and friendship he was shown by the Muslim people of Malaysia and Indonesia and wondered whether the proximity of Buddhism in the countries that surround them affected the people in general. The jewel of Indonesia, Bali, had Hinduism prominent, with Buddhism within its own Balinese culture. In India, Hindus and Muslims coexisted, absorbing energy from each other; it was a feeling you got from the people, when you were travelling overland, an energy you could not see.

"I felt it again in the Punjab", he said. "The energy was changing as I entered the Islamic state of Pakistan. The farther west I came, the harsher the land and a harsher religion; well, it seems to suit the climate, and it totally engulfs the people. Now, I am in Europe with its Western Christianity and the big business of spiritual guidance". He had been theorising that people needed to believe in something for their own spiritual well-being, but also there was the need to understand and to respect each other's beliefs. "It works in the Far East", he had concluded.

They were sitting in a park having a farewell picnic when Toby said, "I have been saving you something for this moment", as he produced a liquorice-skinned joint to the surprise and delight of Miles. It blunted the sorrow of their parting; he felt no pain as he set off for Italy on a high. He got a lift to Ljubljana and then another to Trieste, arriving in the early evening; he ignored a gang of intimidating boys on bikes who began to pester him as he was looking for somewhere to make camp. He had just bought some wine; bread rolls and cheese and decided to keep walking away from the road towards the rocks. From his vantage point on the rocks, he had a panoramic view all around. As he looked out over the Mediterranean Sea, he shouted at the seagulls, "I am in Italy, I am Garuda, I am God!".

He had found his camp for the night. It was a beautiful, clear, moonlit night as he took out the wine, bread rolls and cheese. He gazed down on limousines entering a huge, gated mansion. He was at peace with himself, happy where he was but wondered what they would be eating tonight, as he wrapped a bread roll and some cheese in his sarong to keep for breakfast, and into the Hessian bag that he used as a pillow. He finished the wine, embracing the moment, the sea air, the solitude, the peace, feeling privileged to be connected to the vast universe he could see above his head in all its splendour, then he wrapped himself in his poncho and fell asleep. During the night, he thought he felt some movement and put it down to the sea breeze, but as the dawn was breaking, he opened his eyes to see a rat running away with a bread roll in his mouth. To his horror, he found his breakfast gone from his pillow; the rat had gnawed its way through the Hessian bag and two layers of sarong, before taking off with the food.

He had seen a lot from the back of a truck and that would continue when it took two lifts to Padova and another to Milano before he arrived at a trailer park as the night was drawing in. It had been a progressive but tiring day, and he was happy to be bedded down under a trailer. He was up as dawn was breaking and found an outside tap to have a quick wash, then walked for many miles till a lift on the back of a motorbike took him to Lugano in Switzerland. He was dropped off at a roadside cafe where the Easy Rider, who called himself Luca De Udderway, treated him to breakfast. This was different country, such a contrast to the arid deserts he had been through such a short time ago: the lake was magnificent, and the scenery continuous on the road to Lucerne.

After Luca had left him, he got a lift without having to move from a couple at the next table, and they dropped him off as darkness was descending. He found a wood pile on somebody's farmland that he arranged into a sleeping shelter. As it was dark he did not realise he was sharing the field with a bull; it was the first light of day that he saw the bull, which hurried him up and away on the road to Basel before he could be discovered by the farmer...or the bull.

He had many Swiss friends he could call on but not in Basel. Why was he here? he began to wonder. The road had taken him. *I better be on the right road tomorrow,* he told himself. It was night and he was drawn to a shop with a colour television prominently displayed in the window. He was mesmerised; he had never seen colour TV before. *What else has happened while I have been on my journey?* he mused. He had been oblivious of what had happened in the world since he left Darwin.

Finding somewhere to sleep was his immediate concern; he could see people gathered by a circular bandstand in the park and wandered over. They were people of similar ilk and were all considering using the bandstand as shelter for the night. Fun began when a joint was sparked up, then some bread and fruit appeared and everybody shared. Feeling secure in each other's company, they shared stories, and someone even sang a song; Romany talking, it was like a gypsy gathering.

Bern was the direction he was told to take, and he made an early start like all the others, having to walk a long way before getting a lift to the capital. He smiled when he saw the Gillam Font of Knowledge Academy building but reckoned Gilly would still be away and plodded on. It was the same again leaving Bern; with lifts hard to come by, he ploughed on till it had become dark. He was sitting on his bag at the side of the road with his thumb out when a car stopped that was going the other way.

"You look in trouble. Jump in", said the driver, explaining to Miles that few vehicles would be going that way at night, and he better come with him. He introduced himself as Manon Amishon and he shared a house with other students.

"Call me Garuda", said Miles, smiling gratefully as he got in. They were soon driving up to a chalet with lights coming from the windows. "Namaste", a bowing Miles said as Manon introduced him to his three surprised housemates, insisting everyone speak English. Everybody was curious and bombarded him with questions, but it was when Miles asked where they studied that his acceptance was assured. "At the Gillam Font of Knowledge Academy", came the reply which had Garuda saying, "Bollic… you must know Bollic Shmeller". Of course they did and were delighted with the stories from Kathmandu and the PWC.

I have been saved again, thought Miles, *a traveller in distress, taken in and given food and shelter.* They told him he had taken the wrong road leaving Bern, which meant he was taking the long route to France. Manon drove him to Lausanne in the morning and showed him which direction to take. They waved goodbye, and Miles's next stop would be Besancon, in France.

Once again it was hard-going; maybe it was the way he looked. But he still carried on with the will to survive getting stronger, as he was now in France and his destination was getting closer. He made it to Dijon and a suitable spot in the park to bed down. He had been enjoying his nights under the stars, having been fortunate with the weather. He was on the road early as he had to keep moving and Auxerre was where he was heading. Knowing he was getting closer to his goal, he was enjoying the walks in between lifts. The weather was fine, life was fine. He would sing, "Keep right on to the end of the road"; if he got a lift, great, if not, no worries, he was just enjoying being alive and breathing the air. *This is life.*

It took two days to reach Auxerre. After once again taking the wrong road, he would take a lift off anybody going anywhere and ended up in the town of Montbard. It was an enchanting town with a wonderful and peaceful park, where he found a suitable area to bed down. In the morning, he freshened up by the riverside before heading out of town, in what he thought was the right direction. He walked for miles, which was fine but slow, and after two short lifts he made Tonnerre before nightfall. Looking for somewhere to camp was always an adventure, and he spotted a cabin used by the road workers. *This will do nicely*, he said to himself as he eased open the door to reveal enough space for him to bed down. He was awoken in the morning by the workmen, who chased him out, not at all happy with their hut being used as a hotel.

He got a lift early and he passed through Chablis before reaching Auxerre. He walked slowly to the outskirts, wondering how Toby and Hextra were getting on while he was in their town. After passing through Chablis, he knew he was in wine country. *A drop of Burgundy would be nice*, he thought, as he pressed on to the lovely town of Joigny. He had noticed since crossing into France that there were many churches and cathedrals. He had seen temples and mosques, but now churches were prominent, and they all believed that theirs was the true faith. Miles was contemplating this question when considering, *Can they all be right?* All religions had a moral code to follow, so they had all played a major role in civilisation.

A night on the bank of the river Yonne was his intention until he saw a vineyard and decided to kip under the vines. He was up early with the sun, and before he could be detected, he was off. Still finding lifts hard to come by, it took the whole day to reach Sens. He was weary but still the adrenalin was high as he camped down again in a park. He was moved off the park bench in the morning by the police, who treated him as a vagrant, then they pointed him in the right direction for him to head for Paris. He had no money at all, and his main concern was to cross the English Channel.

Jacques will sort me out, I'm sure, thought Miles, and he was fortunate to get an early lift into Paris. Jacques had given Miles the address of a blues club he would often visit, and people would know how to find him: Rue de Rouen, Vincennes. Jacques had drawn a sketch of how to find it. From where he had been dropped off, he walked for hours, until at last there it was, Club Bohemian. He was tired and hungry when he sat at a table outside the club, and a young waitress came over and spoke.

"*Oui, Monsieur?*"

"*Bonjour*, can I have a drink of water, please? *Merci. Aqua*", he said shyly. She came back later with a tray and placed his glass of water, a plate of bread, cheese, an apple and a bottle of wine on the table.

"You look weary and hungry", she said in English, smiling all the time. "My name is Wyda, Wyda Wayke. How else can I help you?" She was a very pretty girl and so comely in her frumpy clothes. Miles would eat and drink in the manner of a ravenous beast as he told her of his friend Jacques.

"I know who he is", she said. "You must be Itchy Balls, he told me about you. I know him very well. He has temper."

"That's him, no doubt. We got the right man. I have his number, could you phone him for me? I would be grateful", said Miles with a despairing look of a humble traveller and a voice to match. She was delighted to make the phone call and Jacques arrived a half an hour later. He picked Wyda up in the air as Miles shouted, "Jacques put her down!" and they all laughed as the friends embraced.

"Jacques, I have no money. I need to sell my chillum to get to England", said Miles. There were frowns from Jacques and Wyda, as they made their way inside the club. Miles's presence brought inquisitive glances, and when he dug into his bag to bring out the sandalwood chillum to show Jacques, inquisitive glances changed to admiring ones as great interest was shown. Jacques felt responsible for Miles but also embarrassed as he was flat broke himself and had nowhere for him to stay. Wyda came over with another bottle of wine and told Jacques it was on his tab, which he readily agreed to. Along with her came Dominic De Chateau, a friend of Jacques, enquiring about the chillum. Miles was now quite willing to sell the only thing of any value in his possession to afford a ticket over the last hurdle of his extraordinary journey. The intricately carved sandalwood chillum was inspected, and an offer of a US ten dollar bill and seven francs was made. *Oh well, when needs must*, he reflected, and a deal was done.

"Would you like to share a christening bowl?" said Dominic. "You may show technique."

"Delighted", said Miles and after the chillum had been passed around, Jacques made an observation to Miles that Wyda did not smoke and that's why she was Wide awake.

"Ha", said Wyda, pointing at Miles. "You can stay on the couch at my place around the corner, I finish in ten minutes."

Miles was weary. "I could sleep like a log", he told Jacques.

"I will be around in the morning", he replied.

Wyda led the way to her apartment where Miles collapsed on the couch and was out like a light, much to the dismay of Wyda, until the morning when she wakened him to take a shower before breakfast. Jacques was around in a borrowed car that he had to take back in an hour. "I can get you to the right road if we leave now", he said. Wyda and Miles embraced without speaking, just smiling at each other as the car moved away.

"Sleep well?" said Jacques with a wry smile on his face.

"Oh fine, just fine, like a log", said Miles smiling.

It was a rackety, old, odd-shaped Citroen with a funny gear shift that Miles had not seen before. *Very French*, he thought. After driving for a half hour, the car came to a stop and Miles reluctantly got out; he was sad to be leaving his friend but also eager to carry on.

"We have had many adventures together, *mon ami*, and we could have more, maybe South America next year. We must meet again…send me a card", said Jacques, waving goodbye and leaving his friend on the road to Dunkerque and the ferry.

He got a lift straight to the ferry and managed to get a ticket to Dover, as they accepted his ten dollars and seven francs, arriving at the white cliffs just before dark. He jumped up and down before he knelt and kissed the ground after passing through his last customs post. *I am back in Blighty, but not home yet*, Miles told the flea-bitten dog that was sniffing about looking for food like he would be. He walked into town with a growling stomach; he was famished, he had been able to smell the food on the ferry, making his hunger even worse. The food was so near but so far. He stopped at a shop window and was once again mesmerised by a colour TV on display.

"Hey, you look hungry. You want to eat?" said a young guy at his shoulder.

"What, are you kidding me?" said Miles.

"No", he replied, "we are on a free meal on the firm. Come on over". So they walked over to a Chinese restaurant where five of his workmates were all happy to share the food. Curiosity was in abundance at the sight of this ravenous traveller shovelling rice into his mouth as fast as he could, a trick from Sumatra. They were fun-filled and friendly workmen, working out of town. They were intrigued with Miles who kept them amused with stories of his travels, and his name brought the usual hilarity with one of the men offering Miles some talcum powder. The fun was continuous but then they were concerned as to where he would sleep that night and offered him some floor space at their boarding house, which Miles gratefully accepted.

In the morning, the landlady did not mind and set a place for him at breakfast. The men wished him luck as they went off to work, and Miles strode off up the road, refreshed. He thought back to Madame Pistake, the palm reader in Bangkok; she had said he was a chosen one, protected by a Divine spirit. Could it be true, that rescue came from nowhere? *Food and shelter given to a traveller in distress once again…I will see what Andy thinks.* He hitched a ride to Brighton, arriving in the early afternoon and knocked on the door of Andy Kister.

"Hello, is Andy at home?" asked Miles to the elderly lady who opened the door.

"Andrew is not here at present, who are you?" she replied, unable to disguise her surprise at the sight of this earthy person.

"My name is Miles. I'm a friend of Andy's from Thailand. He asked me to look him up when I made the UK."

"Oh, do come in and forgive me for my abruptness…I was not expecting such an interesting-looking individual on the doorstep. I am Andrew's mum. I'll make a nice cup of tea, phone Andrew and tell him you are here."

Andy arrived home soon after, full of smiles and congratulations and eager for stories of his adventure. After a lovely meal prepared by his mum – who was so focused on what Miles had to say, trying to gain an insight of her son's activities (Miles was careful not to say anything incriminating) – they went off to the pub for more detailed accounts of the journey. They were joined in the pub by Andy's friend, Davin Cheecode, who was eager to meet Miles after hearing of his journey.

"Do you remember the mystic palm reader, Andy, and what she meant by the special one?" asked Miles. "I have had some charmed experiences, almost magical. Do you think there could be anything in what she said?"

"Ah, Madame Pistake, there is something in it. What she said about the *M* in your palm, it does signify something special. I looked into it, it means you are courageous, and I can vouch for that. You are hardworking, but spiritually it indicates a balance between the inner self and the outside world."

Davin did not have much to say but hung on to every word these two old friends said, fascinated by the stories being told. He also bought the beer and drove Miles to London the next day. In the morning, Miles was again gracious as he thanked Andy's mother for the hospitality. She had not been ready for the encounter, happy in her own world. It had been a shock, but she had been pleasantly surprised with Miles personality and reminded herself not to judge a book by its cover and smiled as Davin opened the car door for him. Andy had given Miles five pounds, which he promised to repay in a card at Christmas

"That should help you get home", he said.

Chapter Eight

———cMɔ———

England

Earls Court, London, and Miles was quietly reflecting on life around him. He was sitting in a pub looking out at the world going by in front of his eyes at such a pace he wanted to shout at it to slow down. The calling for home was strong now. As he looked in his journal, there were sketches and addresses of people he had met on the way that he could call on.

Ah, Loostea, shall I ring her? No, l will go see her, he decided. *Yes, I better see her. She had been very insistent.* He was rambling on to himself. *There must be a story about the parcel. I have carried it a long way now and it has not caused me any trouble and now my job is done, I can free myself of this responsibility. Yes, she has some explaining to do.*

He could see the tube station through the window of the pub and thought that could be fun, having never been on a tube train before. He decided to finish his pint and head for the tube, and go find Loostea. He studied the underground map in the busy station and saw he had to change at the Embankment from the green line to the black. *That seems easy enough*, he thought, as he looked about at people who knew what they were doing and where they were going. He was in no hurry compared to the urgency of those around him, and he was proud of himself, as he found Camden Town without a hitch. There were detailed directions and a sketch of how to get there from Camden station to her apartment; she did not want him to get lost.

He found the address easy enough and rang the bell to the top floor flat. A curtain moved; he thought he heard a shriek when soon after the door opened with a cry, "Come in, quickly". The door closed and from behind, an overjoyed Loostea flung her arms around him crying, "Itchy, oh Itchy, I am so happy to see you". They climbed the stairs to the second floor and her two-bedroom flat. He was met with the smell of incense burning in front of a shrine to Buddha. Displayed around the room were souvenirs of her travels: a picture from Bali hung over the fire, like the one Miles had sent home in his rucksack. A batik from Java covered the wall opposite and other interesting artefacts were clearly visible. *Aha!* He spotted a "Man in a Barrel". *I did not know she had been to Chiang* Mai; he mused. All the time Miles was observing his surroundings, she was making coffee and never stopped talking about his journey.

She placed a cup on the coffee table, and they were both seated when she said, "Have you still got it?"

"If you mean the package, yes, it has not been out of its pocket since I left Penang. Now then, tell me what this is all about", said Miles in a voice she could not ignore.

She started, "Well, when we were in Jakarta—"

"—we?" interrupted Itchy.

"My flatmate. Who you know", said Loostea, with mischief in her voice as a door opened and surprise exploded over his face.

"Hi Itchy, how you been?" said Valentine. As a stunned Miles rose to his feet, his face filled with joy and wonder as they both embraced.

Miles said, "What is going on?"

Loostea was about to pour whiskey into their coffees when Miles put his hand over the cup, saying, "Maybe not yet, I am still recovering", as they all sat down. He was itching to ask a lot of questions but would wait and see what unfolded.

Loostea began, "First, we would like you to keep the package for another six months". Miles's eyes opened wide at this bombshell and after a slight pause she continued, "You see, it is a condition of Grandfather's will. It contains documents that must be produced at three o'clock on the day of Friday, 26th April, next year. However, there is a Chinese consortium who we believe are trying to prevent that from happening. Val is my cousin, and we were both at our eccentric grandfather's will reading in Adelaide, along with three of Granddad's Chinese business associates. I say eccentric, because the package you have was produced and presented to us as part of the terms and conditions of the will. The documents are in fact the second part of the will, to be delivered intact by a blood relative to a solicitor in London on the given date. If that does not happen, the will becomes invalid and his Chinese business associates will absorb his shareholding in a casino. It all sounds very fishy. There is a swindle going on and we needed to find out how to expose it. Nobody knows what mystery the package holds but if it can be kept safe and produced on the day, we feel it could reveal the truth and secure our inheritance".

Miles was waiting to come in and said, "It is better I did not know, if people have been after it. Have they?"

She answered, "You were being watched from the moment you left the hospital in Penang". Surprise broke out again on Miles's face as he became even more attentive.

"The plan changed when Val, who had been carrying it, had his room ransacked in Jakarta. Fortunately, he had it on his person, as he knew he was being watched. When we met up in Jakarta, I had told him that we were close; also, that you were heading for the UK, and that we needed an alternative plan. We were both being watched and I suggested Val go to Medan. I knew where you would be staying, and Val could explain our predicament to you."

"The hepatitis was not part of the plan", said Val. "I was really crook, as you know, and had to trust that Loostea could rescue the situation in Penang."

"What was in the parcel that Sun Tin Wong took away?" said Miles.

"That was magic mushroom powder for his soup. I had told him exactly what to expect when he went to see you, so he would know the feel. It also had a sticker with his name on it. I had made up the decoy parcel in Bali with the magic mushroom powder that Val had promised Sun Tin Wong. I was going to tell you in the hospital but decided you would be safer if you did not know, and I could take them on a false trail."

"How did they know I was carrying the package?" said Miles.

"I guess it was from them watching me visit you in hospital. I was under constant surveillance, it could only have been that, but once you were out of Maylasia and then Thailand, I knew you would be safe. There were people looking out for you all the time. Ugli Twat reported your incident in Chiang Mai, Mr Chance told me that the village chief had saved a situation, you were unaware of. Then there were the gubbons in Kuala Lumpur. Val was the hero there of something you knew nothing about and Sing Song in Penang. Do you remember the Hat? Well, he and his mate could well be in the UK, and he knows you. They are a hapless pair, but we still need to be on our guard. Snow White gave a comprehensive report from Vientiane that I did not need in such detail. However, I knew you were closer to being in India and hoped you would take your time. Scouse would see you safely on your way."

He had been unaware so many people were involved; it had startled him and now he wanted to dig deeper.

"Why did you not just fly or sail?" queried Miles.

"From the moment we left the office we were being followed", said Val. "We stopped for a pie floater from the mobile pie shop and to discuss the events of the meeting, when we noticed the gubbons. That was a name Granddad would give anybody who did something stupid. These two Chinese blokes, one with a distinctive hat that looked like a collapsed multicoloured turban with a brim, were watching our every move. We had to shake off these two gubbons somehow. Yes, we did consider both of those options, but not for long. We had no time, we had to move fast. It would take too long to get to sailing, and while flying was an option, we had to lose the gubbons, quickly. Quite frankly, we did not know what to do, but after a quick debate we decided to split up, but first we would drive to Alice Springs."

Val continued the story. "That was a tough journey, but we could see we were not being followed. We got to Alice thinking we were safe, when we saw the gubbons at the airport, where Loostea had booked a flight to Darwin. This was where we were going to split up anyway. I would take the car and drive to Darwin, taking the package with me, and staying out bush until I heard from Loostea."

"The gubbons turned up in Darwin", said Loostea, "which has a strong Chinese community. It was not long before my lodgings were searched and when they found nothing, they waited months for Val to arrive".

"I had spent my time writing travel stories for the adventure-holiday magazines I work for in New Zealand", said Val. "I stayed in the bush town Katherine, until Loostea contacted me via the post office. I then drove to Darwin, sold the car and we flew to Bali. It was then that I thought, by going overland to the UK, they would surely not follow. That did not happen, so in Jakarta we hatched a plan that did not work, and here you are, the man who saved the day without knowing."

"One more thing. What is so special about the date? Why all this intrigue and being chased across the globe?" questioned Miles.

"That is more than one thing", said Loostea, smiling. "Well, as for the date, we think that it is the original date that Granddad was to sign the new partnership document. The intrigue is what is in the package; it must hold some secret that could damage our Chinese friends. They have been after the package from the beginning… Why else would they pursue us in this way? It must contain something that will expose or incriminate them if it arrives."

Val continued, "Granddad was a great character; he and Grandma were opal miners in Andamooka, till Grandma died in a tunnel collapse. He was heartbroken and sold the lease before moving down to Adelaide. They had just made a big find before the roof literally caved in. This left Granddad sad and alone, but quite well off. He did not communicate very much over the next few years – an odd letter and a Christmas card to my dad who lives in New Zealand. He and Loostea's mum were his only children".

Loostea joined in with, "Mum married Dad in London and settled down in Brentford. Mum, too, would only receive an occasional letter from Granddad. The last letter she got made her feel anxious. Something had worried her and she tried to contact him. Shortly afterwards, we got news of his passing. Mum was not well, so I flew to Adelaide and Val flew from Auckland to join me for Granddad's funeral.

Val continued, "After the funeral, Dad flew back to New Zealand, giving me instructions to find out what happened".

"Hey, listen, this is a lot to take in. Look at me, I am wrecked", interrupted Miles. "I have been on the road for eight months, I am nearly home and you hit me with this."

"Oh, Itchy, we are sorry, there is not much more to tell. Hear him out, let Val finish", begged Loostea.

"I am in it now… deep in it by the sounds of it", sighed Miles.

Val continued. "We were able to stay in Granddad's house and had use of the car. We realised we had time before the will reading to find out what we could. He had put his money into shares of a casino, which was where he died. The death certificate stated heart attack, and now you know as much as we do", Val finished with a hurried voice.

"Wow", sighed Miles. "I guess I am better off knowing now, not much, but I need to get home, recover, and digest my new found knowledge."

"We are being watched, so get home, stay low and stay alert", warned Loostea. "You are the guardian of our future. It is best not to try and contact us until we meet up on Anzac Day, in the Red Lion by the Cenotaph. It should be safe enough. That is the day before we present the package; we need to be prepared. Good luck, love you."

"Oh, and Lusti said write", squeezed in Val, to perplex Miles even more.

The three of them embraced and Miles slipped out into the dark night, heading for the motorway and home. With all that he had to take in, he had not mentioned his hunger or the fact he had no money, but now he was more concerned about the Hat. The M1 motorway would take him home; he was nearly there. A lift to a service station saw Miles scavenging for food in the cafe area. He watched people eat, hoping they left some morsels for him to clear up. He spent the night at the station and had better luck scavenging in the morning before sharing a cab in a truck going to Middleborough. He jumped out the cab and into the rain. He had been fortunate with the weather. This was the first rain he had felt since being back in Europe, and it was fitting that rain welcomed him home.

I could walk to Whitby from here, he laughed to himself. He did not care how far or wet it was, he just started walking with a broad smile on his face, singing his marching song. He was picked up by a couple going to see Whitby Abbey, the inspiration for Bram Stoker's *Dracula*.

"Our house is just by there", said Miles. "Well, near the start to the one hundred and ninety-nine steps that lead to it."

"Have you been somewhere exciting?" they asked inquisitively, noting his appearance.

"It would take a while to explain, and we are nearly there. In fact, drop me off, I will walk from here. Many thanks. You have been my last lift after being on the road for eight months and ten thousand miles."

They smiled in wonder and watched him as he began strolling down the lane towards his home. He was laughing with every step he took, even gave a little jig as people stopped and stared with bemused smiles. He did not care; he was home.

He breathed in deeply as he knocked on the blue-painted door. He could see his father through the window moving to answer the knock. The door opened, and Miles was greeted with, "Yes?"

"Oh my God!" his father exclaimed as recognition of his travel-weary son beamed across his face. They embraced, with his father crying, "Ma, Ma! Our boy is home". She hurried out of the kitchen, shaking with excitement as she hugged her long-lost son.

"Come in the kitchen. I will put the kettle on, and you can tell us all about how you got here. We thought you might be on the way when a rucksack arrived."

"This calls for the bottle of Port to celebrate", Father cried.

"Tea will be fine", said Miles as he sat at the table. "Ma, I've had an incredible adventure that would take an age to relate, but for now I am tired. I need to recover, have a bath and rest a while. I am physically, mentally, financially and spiritually exhausted!"

Chapter Nine

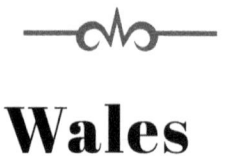

Wales

After being fed, he slept till morning, and after a bath, shave and fresh clothing, he was like a new man. He was certainly not the same boy who left six years before. He had found that survival was life, and life was God, but his spiritual journey was now less important, with the safekeeping of the package being the priority. He checked it was still in its pocket and put the bag in the wardrobe and covered it up.

Down at the breakfast table, Miles was once again enjoying Ma's cooking when his sister Nobald came in. She beamed with excitement as she gave him a big hug, saying, "You look like you need that breakfast".

"Do not worry, I will soon fatten him up", said Ma.

"I need a job, Ma. I want to pay my way", Miles said as he continued to eat as if it were his last meal.

"There is a barman's job going at the White Horse if you want it. My fiancé, Fred, is leaving", said Nobald.

"That sounds perfect. I will get a haircut and see the boss. Your fiancé, you say, Fred?" prompted Miles.

"Yeah", replied Nobald, "Fred Eagle".

Miles got the job and worked as many hours as he could. He was popular with the locals, with many knowing him as a boy. The buxom barmaid in a short skirt – Betty Beautiful, as she was known – would keep the amorous Miles happy, and he used the cosy friendship to ask her to keep an eye out for two Chinamen whom he wanted to avoid.

Christmas came and there had been no sign of the gubbons. The job had worked out well; he had even bought a ridiculously cheap old Ford Escort from a customer. Christmas was always special for Miles and this year even more so as he was home. Pa exclaimed that Miles had received the most cards of anyone, and from all over the world. Miles thought about Christmas and what it meant to him, as a non-believer.

This is it, he reckoned as he picked up the cards. Reconnecting with family and friends. It would be easy to drift away without this practice.

He opened a card from Andy Kister with special wishes from his mum, and then there was one from Charlie, who was back in the US. Demeter had sent a picture of herself; so had Wyda, bringing pleasant thoughts to his mind. Jacques had been enthusiastic in suggesting they both go and explore the ancient historical sites of Mayan and Inca civilisations in Mexico; he was reading up on the Yucatan where they existed, saying there were lots of cultures to explore in South America and would be in touch. The People's World Council members had all fulfilled their promise of sending cards, as did Paddy, Scouse, the Mutt and Froggy and many others that he had not expected, like Robin Banks who now ran a homeopathic clinic, Mary Anbright, Toby and Hextra. It was good to hear from Gude, who had successfully cleared himself of any involvement in the Red Army Faction and was now forging an honest living in a car factory. He had signed off with "Keep Right on to the End", thinking they were unexpected and appropriate words of encouragement. Freddy had sent a letter with bank details and a new price list.

It was New Year's Eve and Miles was busy behind the bar when he spotted the gubbons walk through the door.

"Oh no", was his first reaction as he momentarily froze, he then turned and slipped out of sight. He called Betty over while staying out of sight and told her they were here.

"Who? Oh, those Chinese guys. Don't worry, I'll get rid of them".

Miles had been pointing in their direction as they were speaking. The Hat was not hard to miss, and as she walked over to them, she was pointing to the exit while politely informing them of a private New Year's party. They were reluctant to leave, carefully scanning the hotel bar for any sign of Miles.

A relieved Miles said, "Thanks, Betty, but now I am in a spot of bother, I will have to leave. You see I have something they want; I must keep it out of their clutches for a while longer yet. I do not want my family involved or you, so I cannot say too much. What you do not know, you cannot tell. If you are asked, you know nothing, but for now, I need to get paid up and leave. I will explain when I get back".

Miles was now on the alert to being followed. He would have to move fast, but where to? *I will go to Liverpool and see Scouse; he is involved, and he can help me shake off these gubbons. How did they find me?* he was thinking. *And what the hell is in that package?*

Miles hugged Betty then hugged the shadows on the way home, slipping in through the back door. In the morning he was washed and packed, ready to go, as he went downstairs to his startled mother.

"Happy New Year, Ma", he said, giving her a hug. "Ma, I must go… something has come up. I know this is sudden, but I may be moving about a bit. I will explain when I return. In the meantime, don't say anything to any Chinamen."

It was a wintery morning, and Miles was well covered up as he once again slipped out through the back door carrying the precious parcel in his bag.

Ma sat down unable to move, "He's gone", she exclaimed.

"Gone where?" said Pa as he shuffled into the kitchen.

"I don't know, just gone and he said we are not to talk to any Chinamen. Heavens above, what is going on?" She sat wondering what it could be that Miles was mixed up in and why he had to leave so suddenly, when there was a knock on the door. Ma and Pa looked at each other before Pa went and opened the door to find two Chinese on the doorstep, one with a distinctly colourful hat. They enquired about Miles, but Pa would only shake his head without speaking to every question they asked until they got fed up and left, but not far, as they sat in their car watching the house.

Ma was now distraught, crying, "What shall we do, Pa? I am so worried".

"We do nothing. We can be thankful he got away when he did. That was close. And we can pray."

A bitter wind was blowing off the North Sea as Miles climbed into his car that he kept behind the pub – the old banger had character and took a while to warm up – before he set off for Scarborough, the next town along the coast, then he would head west to York. *How did they find him?* he kept wondering as he drove along, while keeping a close eye in his mirror. He stopped in York because it was a beautiful city with an enormous past. The historic city was fascinating to Miles. As he sat in a quaint old coffee shop staring out of the window, he imagined all the people who had passed by through the centuries, while all the time watching out for the gubbons. He was satisfied they could not know where he was going; he had not told anybody.

I am going to have to make myself scarce for a few months, but how? I hope Scouse has some good ideas.

He drove to Manchester and then down the East Lancashire Road to Liverpool. The car was doing well apart from the dodgy brakes, as he travelled along Queens Drive to West Derby and Moscow Drive where Scouse lived. He parked up on the road before walking up the driveway and knocking on the door. He did not have to wait long for it to open and he blurted, "G'day, you Bludger".

A surprised Scouse stuck out his hand to welcome Miles through the door, as he shouted, "Come in, Itchy, come in! It's good to see you still in one piece. You must have a story or you would not be here", he said with a wry grin on his face. "Let's go in the kitchen and you can tell me all about it."

Miles sat down with a sigh, breathed deeply and said, "I am an unfortunate participant in an intriguing mystery I know nothing about, or did not know until I was deep in it. Loostea told me of your involvement, which is why I am here, and because I have two Chinamen on my tail, and I cannot figure out how they found me".

"Well, with a name like yours, that would not have been too difficult, but you have come to the right place. I can put you up while we decide what to do. Mum and Dad won't mind if it's not for too long; they have always said anything over three days is a long time. We need a strategy. Now, how did you get here"?

Miles replied, "I have a car, of sorts, but it is better than I thought; it just keeps going".

"Well, if they are to catch up with you again it will be through the car and its registration", said Scouse, continuing, "I don't think the gubbons are clever enough on their own. They will have someone directing them".

Miles was blunt. "Tell me, how did you get involved with Loostea? She knows a variety of people to call upon."

Scouse was smiling as he replied, "We belonged to a Buddhism correspondence group created by Ugli Twat after he had posted the idea in a travel magazine that both of us responded to, along with Snow White".

Miles broke in with, "Ugli Twat…I met him in Chiang Mai. Aha! That explains the Man in a Barrel I saw in her flat".

Scouse went on, "We were pen pals, if you like, and Ugli Twat had proposed a meeting to be held in Bangkok. Loostea was in Australia, so a convenient date was confirmed to work in with her journey home. That was when you were still in Malaysia. She told us all her story, and that you would be coming through and needed protecting from the gubbons. It sounded intriguing and even more so now. I'm excited just think we are involved in the safety of something we don't know what, and with no mention of any reward, but it just seems right. Oh, I have something for you, won't be a minute".

After a short while, Scouse returned with a parcel, identical to the one still in its pocket in the bag, saying, "Loostea gave me this in Bangkok. She said it might come in useful".

This is another turn-up, Miles thought as he stared at the parcel, saying, "She must have anticipated our meeting up again. What I do know is it will all be over by the end of April. Till then, I must stay low, but I cannot live on fresh air. Any ideas?"

Miles laughed when Scouse said, "Let's go the pub".

At this time of year, Whitby was a quiet town and the gubbons realised the bird had flown. They were having dinner when the Hat said, "Trail gone cold Number Two; we need to make more enquiries. We will ask waiter".

"Excuse me", he asked, "do you know My Balls Itch a Lot?"

An unsuspecting Fred Eagle was smiling when he told them he had not seen Miles and he could have driven somewhere. Their Chinese eyes opened wide as the Hat said, "He has a car".

"Yes", he replied with enthusiasm, giving a detailed description, not realising he was inadvertently placing Miles in peril. The smiling gubbons rose from the dining table in the hotel, thanking the head waiter Fred with a tip, and went into the lobby to make a phone call.

They were sitting in Scouse's local pub, The Jolly Miller, while deciding what to do next. Miles was savouring his pint when he said, "Why am I in this mess? I do not know, but now, I want to know what is in the parcel. I will carry on with your help, Scouse. Are you with me?"

"You bet, all the way. This could be fun… doing something with the prospect of getting nothing, it is spiritual, and I can help as I am self-employed. I do a bit of decorating, a bit of gardening and I fix people's cars, I get work from the local OAP society, doing jobs for the old folk who cannot get about. This leaves me flexible enough to fit in with whatever may lie ahead. Now, Itchy, you may not remember my name, but it is Justin Damood. I'm known as Dam, or Moody, as everybody here is a Scouse."

An amused Miles said, "I will call you Moods… I see problems with Dam. First, we must stay calm and determined. You only fail if you quit; we must keep on going, no matter what".

Scouse was bubbling when he said, "We are now brothers on a quest to nothing, started by that Ugli Twat. Now, I know the bakery in Rathbone Road is looking for drivers. You could get digs in a boarding house I know, and we will be fine".

Miles replied, "Sounds okay, if they accept my Australian driving licence".

They sat for a couple of hours discussing strategy and the next move. The following morning, Miles was successful in getting a job delivering bread to the shops around Liverpool. They told him he could park his car in the yard while he was out in the van. This was ideal, as were the digs in Derby Lane, Old Swan. For two weeks he enjoyed every passing day without sight of the gubbons. He enjoyed the job and the banter with the shop owners; it was always friendly and amusing, and he was confident he would not be discovered.

The Chinese networks around the country had many eyes on the lookout for an E reg green Ford Escort. Fred had given a good description; it was only a matter of time before it was spotted. It was Chinese New Year. Miles had parked too close to the parade celebrating the year of the

Tiger. He had an insatiable lust for learning about distinct cultures, and watched unobserved from a distance, but it was the car that was seen. The gubbons had stayed in Whitby waiting for instructions. The call came, and off to Liverpool they went.

Miles's job was early start and early finish, leaving the afternoon free, and he would meet up with Moods each day in the Jolly Miller. This day would change the direction they had to take. It was the last day of January, and Miles was happy delivering his bread in Old Swan when he saw the Hat. His mouth dropped as he turned his head to avoid being recognised; the gubbons had driven past when Miles was carrying a tray of bread into a shop. He finished his round, all the while tossing ideas around in his head and thought he had the next move if Moods would agree.

"They're here", was all Miles said as he sat down with the pints, leaving Moods to dwell on his words. "However, I have a plan, and with your help we can escape their attentions for a while". Miles went on to explain the sighting of the Hat, and what he had in mind. "I have a friend in Ireland", he said. "You know Paddy. They could not trace me over there, and in the meantime, you take the car and lead them on a merry dance. I will get paid up tomorrow and take the night ferry to Dublin."

An enthusiastic Moods said, "Now that is a cunning plan. That will work – I can meet up with you later after I lose them, and I know how. You know, this is getting better all the time".

After a couple of drinks, they had expanded the plan. With the cold weather, they would both wear duffel coats to help confuse the expected arrival of the gubbons; Moods would take the dummy parcel with him without concealing it too much to ensure they follow him and the car. Miles was beginning to enjoy the drama while Moods was positively excited, already working on diversion tactics.

The following afternoon, with Moods driving, they filled up with petrol at a station near to Chinatown, taking their time in the process. They could feel the eyes upon them and saw a hasty phone call being made. Miles took a leather satchel bag out of the boot – it had a pocket on the front with a flap that would hold the dummy parcel – and handed it to Moods, remonstrating its importance. Moods placed the bag on the back seat as they both got back into the car and drove off.

A Cork in a Storm

"I think that worked", Miles said to the excited Moods who was concentrating on the moment and loving it.

They drove around until at last, Moods declared, "I think we got them. A few more turns to make sure, then we will head for the Mersey tunnel". The plan was to lose them in Birkenhead. Miles would hop on the ferry back to Liverpool and then onto the ferry to Ireland.

The gubbons had arrived in Liverpool with instructions to contact Foo kin Hu in Chinatown. He was dressed in black pyjamas and said he would tell them when the car was sighted. The Hat had become obsessed with finding them; he had a grudge to settle after what happened in Fang, how he had been humiliated by the villagers. They had scooped him up in a net and left him hanging all day. He remembered Penang and Kuala Lumpur and how he had ended up in hospital on both occasions. This time it would be different; he would not rest until he had the bag containing the parcel.

He was sitting with Number Two by the window in a tea parlour observing the traffic, when they were beckoned from outside by Foo Kin Hu and were told the car had been found and the parcel was in the satchel on the back seat. Number Two was driving as they sped in the direction that Foo Kin Hu pointed. It was not long before the Hat screamed, "There they go. Now do not lose them – we have got them this time!" They entered the long and winding tunnel in pursuit of their prey, but the delay at the toll booth in Birkenhead allowed their prize to escape. Not having picked up the trail after a half hour, they decided to keep watch near the tunnel entrance.

Miles sang, "Hey Mood, you know it is a year since I left Darwin and the adventure continues…every day is an adventure". Miles was reflecting as they sat hidden by the Wallasey docks; they were happy the way the plan was going and wished each other good luck as Miles got out at the Seacombe ferry. Moods drove back towards the tunnel and beamed with joy when he spotted the gubbons, and they spotted him. He was enjoying himself as he drove back through the never-ending tunnel and out onto Scotland Road, up towards Goodison Park, the home of Everton football club. He passed the ground and was heading for the East Lanc's Road, when he felt the brakes not responding as they should. Miles had warned him of the dodgy brakes and that he would have to take it easy. It was now dark and the gubbons were close on his tail as he approached the

M6 motorway heading north towards Scotland. He knew they had him as soon as he stopped. He would drive to Carlisle thinking that should be far enough away for Miles to escape.

Once into the city, with the gubbons close behind, he pulled over and got out of the car. Slowly walking over to a phone box, he left the bag unattended, and the tempting bait was too much for the Hat to miss as he snatched the bag and took off. It could not have gone any better. Moods was overjoyed but did not relax; they could have opened it. He refilled the tank and drove back to Liverpool.

It was in the early hours when he parked the car in his dad's driveway. He was happy he had not been followed and went to bed delighted with the day's work, drifting off to sleep looking forward to the next day.

"What is that car doing on the drive? Come on, get up. Tell me", said Amin Damood, his disgruntled father. "You will need to move it."

"Sorry, Dad, but can it wait? I am tired, I got home late. I will move it when I get up, promise." His sleep was now broken. *The car has to go*, was his last disturbing thought as he drifted back off to sleep.

The gubbons had sat watching the cars enter the tunnel when the Hat said, "I was right, there they are. Now do not lose them, Number Two; we must not fail this time. Look, there is only the driver…which one get out? They both look the same. I think we will follow the car. Carry on".

"It is good he no drive too fast in dark", said Number Two as they followed Moods from a safe distance waiting for him to stop. The opportunity arose when they had followed him into Carlisle.

"Look, he's getting out. Now is the time. Keep motor running, Number Two." The Hat was fast over to the Escort and quickly lifted the bag from the back seat and dived back into their own vehicle amid cries of "*Qu, Qu, Qu*… Keep going, Number Two! We will pull into the next petrol station and look at our prize".

The Hat took out the parcel to inspect it. "Master give big reward for this. We have done it, Number Two! Now we fill up the tank, drive to Preston, find hotel and phone master in morning. Too late now."

They were up early, and much joy could be heard when the Hat made his call and was instructed to drive straight to Old Compton Street, Soho, London. The Hat was very pleased with himself as he entered the office of M.G.M. Mandarin Games and Magic, Ping Pong Industries. The Hat and Number Two were smiling as the Hat placed the package on the desk, proud of their achievement and hungry for the reward. The smartly dressed Kun Hing Won picked up the package.

"This could mean a big bonus for you", he said smiling, as he began to undo the ribbon from the maroon velvet bag, tearing it off to reveal a book called *The Adventures of Noddy and Big Ears* by Enid Blyton. "You fools! They have tricked you again. Find that car, go back and see if Foo Kin Hu can find it!"

The gubbons were horrified at the disclosure. Feeling rage, combined with shame at their failure, they sheepishly stumbled out of the office as quick as they could. Kun Hing Won looked at the book thinking they chose well, when a slip of paper fell from within the pages which just read, "Namaste", which enraged him even more.

Miles took the ferry across the Mersey to the Pier Head, then walked down to the docks and hopped aboard the night ferry to Ireland. It was a dark wintery night outside, as he enjoyed the cosy surroundings of the lounge bar as the ferry sailed out of Liverpool Bay. He was confident he had boarded undetected as he revelled in the fun atmosphere that reflected how he felt inside, joining in with the singing, expressing his joy of the day, feeling safe and secure.

The lounge had been full of sleeping passengers but was near empty when Miles arose from the bench seat bed and grabbed a coffee before going on deck to look out over Dublin Bay, convincing himself as he spoke to the wind, "They will never find me here". It was a cold grey morning as he walked from the North Wall along the banks of the Liffey to the bus terminal, where he would head west to Galway.

Ireland had always interested him through the music; he felt like he was coming home. It was a beautiful country, but they were having trouble up north. He was confident of any situation that might befall him. He was a survivor, a god; he would be alright coming back into a very Catholic culture. The slow journey across Ireland was an ideal time for reflection. Catholicism was not high on his list of beliefs with credibility, and not worth any more scrutiny; it was fully exposed in his eyes.

I wonder how Paddy is coping back in his hometown after his spiritual journey? I am looking forward to meeting up again. I hope he does not mind.

The countryside was as green as he had been told and the towns full of inviting mystery he would love to explore; his yearning for learning was guiding him onward, through Ballinasloe and Loughrea and onto Galway City. It was fifty miles to Clifden and too late in the day to chance hitching, so he took the bus, thus draining his limited resources, and he was once again counting the coppers. The views turned spectacular after passing through Oughterard and then Maam Cross. The mountains looked down onto a rugged countryside full of challenge and absolute splendour. *Why would anybody want to leave here?* he thought, as the beauty continued along the winding road to find Paddy Fields.

Griffins Bar looks a good place to start, he thought as he walked into the first pub in town. The welcoming smell of the turf fire and the ensemble of local clientele made him feel comfortable, like he belonged there. He ordered a pint of Guinness and asked where he could find Paddy Fields.

"You are in the wrong country, sir. We have the Fields of Athenry and lots of bog. You should try China". The humour was not lost on anybody; they were all still laughing when he went on to say, "Yeah, you look like someone who would know Paddy. He should be in soon. My name's Roy".

Paddy came through the door and screamed, "Itchy!" saving an introduction, as all eyes watched them embrace as old friends would. "I am going to love hearing what stories you have to tell, and why you are here. It must be for a reason."

Moods realised they would have opened the dummy package and would come looking again for the car. He dared not drive it without the brakes being fixed and decided to get them sorted at a local garage. He was told to come back in two days; in the meantime, he would get some funds together and prepare for more drama. He had decided that the dummy package had worked once, and he would make another one. *It may help… who knows?* he reasoned and got to work creating another diversion.

Fu Kin Hu had already been informed of the deception and had set out details of the search when the gubbons arrived. He had a fleet of cars patrolling the city, he told them; it would be found if still in Liverpool. It was located the next day at a garage in Knotty Ash. The gubbons would sit, watch, and wait with renewed confidence of picking up the trail again.

Moods had said goodbye to his dad after borrowing some money and the road map, and before telling him he was on a mission. Amin smiled on hearing of his mysterious venture. He had shown no fear, only excitement; whatever he was doing, he had faith in his son. Moods now walked along Queens Drive and up Prescot Road to the garage, shouldering his trusty rucksack. He was surveying the area as he approached the garage, being alert for anything suspicious. He picked up the car and drove cautiously down the road keeping a watchful eye out for the gubbons. His plan was to visit a friend he had met in Chiang Mai called Trevor Trevor, who had been introduced to him by Ugli Twat and Loostea. Trevor lived in Swansea, so driving through the Welsh countryside would surely reveal any pursuers. This meant he would once again go through the Mersey Tunnel and head for Chester.

He had been aware of a car following him and was happy to see it take another road after coming out of the long and winding tunnel. He felt he was becoming paranoid as cars under suspicion would turn off and make him smile as he arrived in Chester positive and alert. He was confident by the time he reached Wrexham that he was not being followed, then the rain began to fall, and the wipers would not work. He pulled into a lay-by before the next town to tie some string to the wipers; it was going to be a manual operation from now on.

He was getting back in the car when he saw the gubbons pass in a light blue Viva. "Game On!" he shouted and drove a short way to Oswestry, to let the rain reside and consult his road map. He had alternative routes in his head as he took the road to Welshpool; there would be no more stopping as he by-passed the town and headed for Newtown. Now that he knew what car to look out for, he was quite relaxed when the Viva appeared in the rear-view mirror; he was going to show them some country roads. The next plan was to drive to Merthyr Tydfil and lose them on the way. It would take them away from his real destination and give Moods a lot of fun. He wanted to make Swansea before dark and was not going to hang about as he picked up speed and turned off at Newtown for Builth Wells but still could not shake them. He was enjoying himself, knowing there were plenty of lanes ahead to lose them, when a tractor came to his assistance. Managing to put the tractor between himself and the gubbons, he accelerated away, leaving them once again in despair.

The joy of eluding the gubbons again drove him confidently on to Trevor's house in a place called Cockett, on the outskirts of the city. He knew he had the right address as a statue of Buddha adorned the centre of the front garden surrounded by red-leaved shrubs. The house was semi-detached with a driveway up the side, and as Moods parked on the drive, Trevor came out the front door beaming with delight at seeing Moods, who said, "Hi Trev, before we catch up, I would like to hide the car, I have someone on my tail".

"No worries, mate. Drive it up to the back of the house while I get a tarpaulin from the shed."

It did not take long before the Escort was covered and out of sight. Trevor made the tea, and they sat at the kitchen table. Moods began to tell the story so far. An attentive Trevor smiled all through the tale of intrigue and said, "First, you stay here tonight, and we will talk again in the morning after a good night's sleep".

"He is moving, Number Two, you know the plan. We keep out of sight and follow instructions on radio", the Hat said quietly, eager for the chase to begin. Foo Kin Hu was in control; he had his three drivers, Wi, Wot and Wen, well drilled, and the radio contact allowed them to interchange as they followed Moods.

Wot was behind the Escort, as they drove into town and radioed in to say "Subject heading for Mersey Tunnel". Wi and Wen took over in Birkenhead and followed the Escort through a scenic route to Chester; they were then called back by Foo Kin Hu, as it was now the Hat's turn to trail the Escort. The Hat was eager to make up for his mistake. He had been embarrassed and was determined to succeed, but at the moment they had to find out where he was going.

"Maybe we let him stay long way in front, Number Two. He is on main road, easy to follow, but now rain come, maybe get closer."

They were travelling past a lay-by when the Hat shouted, "There he is! Keep going, Number Two. Do not worry; we will wait for him farther up road. Pull in next petrol station".

After filling up the tank they parked, concealed behind a hedge, with Number Two saying, "He be long time, maybe we go back".

The Hat was quick to reply, "No, Number Two, be patient. You will see, he must have gone into last town, he will pass very soon. Look, there he goes! You tell master me very clever. Now keep up and do not lose sight… we must not fail".

A Cork in a Storm

Number Two was doing well to keep up until after they passed Builth Wells and encountered country lanes and a tractor that blocked their path, allowing Moods to escape. After the tractor had turned off into a field, they sped on to Merthyr Tydfil, traversing the town in search of the Escort until the bewildered pair came to a halt where the road would lead to Cardiff or Swansea.

"I think we will go left to Swansea. Go quickly, let us not waste time."

They searched the city for hours, until in desperation, the Hat reluctantly rang the Master and then had to wait by the phone for instructions. In the office of MGM, Kun Hing Won was piecing together the information he had on the movements of their subject. After much deliberation, he concluded the parcel carrier had disappeared on the Irish ferry from Liverpool and his accomplice was off to meet him. He would still send a team to check out Cardiff, but he instructed the Hat to continue the search in Swansea and to stay in Fishguard until further notice, keeping watch on the ferry passengers. They did as instructed, covering every nook and cranny, only a statue of Buddha catching the eye on the drive to Fishguard to begin their surveillance.

The smell of bacon frying had Moods up early and willingly made the tea and toast. They were sitting at the kitchen table when Trevor said, "I would like to go with you. I have no immediate plans. We can go on my motorbike and take the late-night ferry from Fishguard to Rosslare. It sounds too exciting for me to miss". Mood's jaw kept opening wider with every word of this unexpected offer to which he gladly agreed. Trevor would be an ideal companion. He seemed to have a few bob, too; he had a house.

It was an interesting journey as a pillion rider while looking out for the gubbons, and when on the approach road in Fishguard, Moods saw the pale blue Viva. The crash helmets and scarf-covered faces provided a perfect disguise as they rode undetected past the gubbons keeping watch at the ferry, who took no notice of the motorbike.

Chapter Ten

Ireland

The five-hour crossing to Rosslare was not rough enough to prevent them from sleeping in the lounge, ready for a drive to Cork when the ferry docked. Trevor was proving to be a major asset; he talked over breakfast in a cafe about how he would often visit Cork just to go to the market on a Saturday, and of the friends he had in County Clare, where they could stay that night.

"But first you must kiss the Blarney Stone. It will bring you luck on this adventure."

Luck, Moods was thinking, *I have a bucket full already. I do not want to break the spell, but we are here now; it must be done.*

They climbed the steps to the top of the castle, bending over backwards to kiss the stone, and after receiving his certificate, they took off for Limerick. Moods was loving every minute of his good fortune. *Am I a chosen one like Itchy?* he was thinking, as he enjoyed the experience of being a pillion rider and just being alive in an adventure.

After a short stop in Limerick, they travelled on to Ennis. Moods was embracing every mile along the twisting road to a town called Feakle. Gwladys Street and her husband, known as Happy, lived in a small, isolated cottage outside of town, and Happy came out to meet them as they drove up.

A Cork in a Storm

"Be Jasus, will ya look at im! An' who's dat ya have wid ya? Come in, come in."

Trevor had first met them at the market in Cork and had even spent last Christmas with them, adding a Buddhist flavour to this spiritual festival of friends. After dinner, with much talk of the mystery quest, their hospitality extended into the pub, where they enjoyed good cheer, music, and song. Moods had been impressed by his hosts as he thanked them heartily while, after a traditional cooked breakfast, they waved goodbye and headed for Galway.

The city was full of charm and character as they roamed the streets until they found the road to Clifden that would lead them to Miles. Excitement and joy engulfed Moods, as the roads would only allow them to travel at a leisurely pace, stopping often to admire the stunning scenery, while at Maam Cross they had a drink at the bar. Come shop, come petrol pump, come undertaker and post office, until at last, after viewing the most stupendous scenery, they arrived in a town nestled within a theatre of natural beauty. An eventful week had passed since Moods left Miles to go on his own adventure, and he was thrilled when he saw him coming out of Griffins Bar.

"Pull in", he told Trevor, and he took off his helmet in front of a delighted Miles. A quick embrace saw Miles about turn and lead them through the bar doors, where they squeezed into the corner where Paddy was standing on this busy Friday evening. There was great fun, with Moods being proud and delighted to introduce Trevor Trevor and meet up with Paddy again. Trevor was already clued up on Miles when he said of Itchy, "That's a name to keep quiet". He then went on to offer to buy dinner; they would go to the Celtic Hotel and discuss what to do next.

The attractive Bridget popped her head out from the kitchen door to survey the night's customers and was surprised to see Miles, who had not impressed her after she'd seen him falling out of Griffins one night. He, on the other hand, was keen to make her acquaintance. Miles had been staying in a self-contained flat attached to the house of Paddy's parents, who rented it to him cheap, being out of season and a friend of Paddy, so Moods could now share. Trevor had told them he would book a room at the hotel and leave in the morning.

"I will be back in time for us to make plans to complete this journey, of which I am excited and proud to belong to this brotherhood". They raised their wine-filled glasses to the success of the quest. They were now four…what could go wrong?

There was no luck in watching the passengers, which annoyed the Hat even more; he was embarrassed and needed to redeem himself. "Tomorrow, we investigate house with Buddha in garden. Number Two, we need to find something."

"Why you wear that hat? We keep losing them because they see you looking like a traffic light! You need to be less easy to see", said Number Two.

"My hat has magic power to make me clever. I only pay Zig-Zag twenty-five dollar. He say to wear it all the time to be very clever".

They drove to Cockett in the morning and knocked on the door of the house with the garden Buddha. Finding nobody at home, they walked up the drive to behold the tarpaulin-covered car at the back of the house. After lifting the tarpaulin to reveal the Escort, they quickly returned to the car all smiles. The Hat was once again pleased with himself as they drove back to their hotel to report his find to the Master, who took down the address and then instructed them to keep a discreet watch on the house and report any movements.

The Master banged down the phone in frustration while digesting the new finding and thinking back to how it all started. Five years had passed since Grandpa Anweir had walked into the office of MGM in King William Street, Adelaide. He had proposed a venture of a Wild West casino, using his own sizable investment; however, he needed the business expertise of people connected to the gambling industry and he felt MGM fit the criteria. Mandarin Games and Magic provided all forms of gambling and gaming requirements; they also ran a TAB bookies' office. There were three directors of Ping Pong Industries: Li Ying Tung, an attractive lady who was the glamorous front to their operations; himself, Kun Hing Won; and Zig-Zag, the magician – he was an illusionist but was into horse race fixing and illegal Chinese medicine.

The venture was a casino with the theme of a Wild West saloon. Guests would enter through swing bar room doors; there was a roulette wheel, waitresses dressed as cowgirls, a piano player and slick-looking croupiers dealing poker and blackjack. A proposal was agreed that Grandpa would have no practical input but would have a fifty per cent shareholding in the casino and five per cent of Ping Pong Industries. Legal documents were drawn up and the enterprise was soon up and running, becoming an immediate success. After two years of harmony and profitable business acumen, Grandpa Anweir had recouped most of his outlay and was happy sitting in the saloon sipping his beer and smoking his pipe. The meeting he had with Li Ying Tung and Zig-Zag revealed that Grandpa had been looking into the accounts; it was time for Grandpa to go.

Zig-Zag had said, "Leave it to me", but instead they conspired to devise a plan that would excite Grandpa enough for him to accept a challenge. Ping Pong Industries had an interest in a casino in Soho, London, and they had asked Grandpa to go to England and set it up the same as in Adelaide. The incentive was, he would take fifty per cent of the profits after the conversion, however, the condition was he would have to have it up and running by the last Friday in April 1974. That would have to be confirmed in person at the office of a solicitor in London on the same date, after which he could return to Australia. They had written into the document, in small print, that Cornelius Anweir would forfeit all his holdings in the casino back into Ping Pong Industries if the terms were not met. Grandpa had agreed, stating he would use the time to visit his son in New Zealand and then a cruise to the UK to see his daughter and still have plenty of time to set up the operation. They all signed the document that would have to be produced again in London as part of the contact, and when Grandpa died, they thought they had a legal right to his shares. The outcome of the will reading was an unexpected drawback, but they did not think it too much of a problem to overcome, until now.

I should have left it to Zig-Zag in the first place.

April had arrived. Miles and Moods had found work with a sandblasting company working on the local church; it kept them solvent, as they loved every minute of living in Connemara. Miles thought it was the Shangri-La of the Northern Hemisphere; he had quickly melted into the community and had developed a close relationship with Bridget from Ballyconneely. However, she said he had better change his name if they were to progress, after seeing an article in the latest edition of the *Connaught Tribune* with the heading: "My Balls Itch A Lot in Raglan Road." It appeared because of his well-received rendition of a song of the same name. Those who did not know, knew now of Mibald Zytchalot in Clifden, but Miles was more concerned of how wide the Chinese network extended.

It was Friday evening and Griffins Bar was as busy as usual. Moods was telling Paddy that if Itchy got hitched up with Bridget, she could become "Bridge Shits a Lot". They were laughing when Miles came over and enquired about the joke, then Trevor walked in to a riotous welcome, which allowed the question to disappear. He was quick to repeat the offer of dinner in the Celtic Hotel and discuss events so far to which everybody readily agreed.

They finished their drinks and walked a short distance to the dining room in the Celtic Hotel. Trevor went on to tell them how he had taken the overnight ferry from Cork to Swansea to avoid the lookouts in Fishguard, how he had approached his house with caution, riding up the drive only to see the tarpaulin on the car had been disturbed, and at once turned around. He was still on the alert as he went back down the street, and there they were: the gubbons in the pale blue Viva, watching the house.

"I was noticed but I was not followed, and I carried on to London to stay in a flat acquired for me by Loostea."

"Loostea, I knew it! What a tangled web she weaves. But you got to love her!" exclaimed Miles.

Trevor smiled at the interruption as he carried on with the tale.

"The flat was just below Loostea and Val, allowing for meetings to go unobserved. I had arranged to meet with Loostea in Chiang Mai, to coincide with our journeys home, you see, I was already involved. Forgive me, Moods, I had to first make sure you would all be safe and secluded. You could not have found a better place to survive undetected, even though they know you are in Ireland."

Miles took out the *Connaught Tribune* and laid it on the table in front of Trevor, who could not miss the heading: "My Balls Itch A Lot." He read the article with horror, as this would surely alert the Chinese.

"This means we will have to move sooner than planned, but I will finish my tale. I took on a role of watching the watchers and what I learned will prove very useful in our quest. I have also had a sidecar fitted to the motorbike for our next move. We may have to make it up as we go along, but we will have to move now – I suggest first thing in the morning".

They discussed the outline plan, and Paddy would be the man to create a diversion when the Chinese arrived, and they did, the next day. Trevor had suggested they go north, as the Chinese would not expect that, so they set out early after breakfast in the Celtic Hotel where Trevor had spent the night. Miles had been able to say goodbye to a tearful Bridget and promised he would return when his quest was complete. He made himself comfortable in the sidecar, excited about what lay ahead and this next stage of the journey.

The boss picked up the phone and rang Foo Kin Hu; he needed somebody in Ireland and instructed him to put his best men on the night ferry to Dublin and for him to come down to London. Nee Ding Lu was assigned to search for Mibald Zytchalot in Ireland, where he would contact Dirty Mary who ran a chip shop in Dublin. She knew everything that went on, but with nothing to go on, it may take a while before they got a lead. Foo Kin Hu left Dim Sum Dung in charge as he drove to London to see the Master; he was keen to advance his position in the firm and would do his best to impress.

He entered the offices of MGM the next morning and sat down with Kun Hing Won to discuss strategy. Foo Kin Hu would recruit enough spies to cover all ports; they needed more eyes to catch their prey. The Master told him he was in for a promotion and a large bonus if he could locate this "My Balls Itch a Lot", and that he would be in charge until the arrival of Li Ying Tung. Business commitments meant he had to go back to Australia. He impressed upon Fu Kin Hu that he must make sure everybody knew who and what they were looking for. Seizing his opportunity to impress, Foo Kin Hu quickly set about co-ordinating, informing and recruiting a team capable of getting the job done.

Zig-Zag met the Master at the airport in Sydney. He was to pick up a consignment of illegal drugs, Chinese traditional medicine and weird herbal concoctions that had been smuggled into the country. It was a lucrative enough business for Zig-Zag to drive to Sydney in his Holden Ute to pick it up. Zig-Zag would accompany the Master at a meeting of the Triads at a strip club in King's Cross. There was much to distract, and Zig-Zag came under the spotlight from the start. The meeting began with Yu Fat Kow, the Sydney Triad *oyabun*, asking him, "Did you eliminate your partner in the casino and why? We know your reputation for making people disappear".

"His death certificate states heart attack", Zig-Zag answered. "However, he had been delving into areas that did not concern him and his demise was a timely convenience."

There was a mistrust developing as the Melbourne *oyabun*, Kwan Tum Leep, asked, "How close did he get to our operation to warrant such action? This is disturbing".

The Master answered, "We are confident that whatever he found out will not be discovered".

"How can you be so sure? Is there something out there that you have not disclosed?" Yu Fat Kow asked.

The Master was beginning to feel uncomfortable as he replied, "There is a package that may or may not contain material that could embarrass us, which at this moment is in the UK. His grandchildren are the carriers of the package. They must present it in London on the twenty-sixth of April, or they will forfeit any inheritance. We have the whole British network on the case and are close to retrieving it. The package will be in our hands very soon".

There were looks exchanged between Yu Fat Kow and Kwan Tum Leep before Zig-Zag added, "There is nothing that can connect us to his death, and in a week's time we will confirm the whole matter closed".

"A week it is. You will inform us of any changes", said Yu Fat Kow.

The following morning, Kun Hing Won was flying back to Adelaide and Zig-Zag took him to the airport before driving to Canberra. He dropped off part of his lucrative cargo in Canberra and continued with his journey, not realising he had picked up a tail. He had been driving all day and was tired as he drove to Wagga Wagga, where he stayed the night. He was up early the next morning and after delivering more of his illegal goods, he was away on his long drive to Mildura.

Detective Bruce Bruce of the Adelaide police had been on the case of Ping Pong Industries and MGM. The investigation into their activities was well under way when they had been alerted by Mr Frank Leigh that the life of Cornelius Anweir could be in danger. This was news they could not ignore, as Zig-Zag was also under investigation about the disappearance of Slippery Sid, an underworld police informant. When

Cornelius Anweir died, they began to treat it as a murder enquiry; his diary had provided enough information that would just need a little extra support to get convictions and close the whole operation. Detective Owen Fault of the Canberra police had been co-operating with detective Bruce in the surveillance of Zig-Zag. They were both aware of his trafficking in narcotics and other substances and were collecting evidence from every drop Zig-Zag made, before they would co-ordinate a simultaneous bust, along with Detective Blue Bellend of the Victorian constabulary.

Owen Fault rang Bruce Bruce to tell him Zig-Zag was heading for Mildura and should arrive late afternoon. This meant Detective Bruce could lie in wait and follow him to his destination. Zig-Zag duly arrived and Detectives Bruce and Blue Bellend, along with his men, followed him down to a houseboat on the Murray River and observed most of the remaining cargo being unloaded.

"Now is the time, Blue", said Bruce, as he made radio contact between the forces and a co-ordinated series of raids began. As Bruce, Bellend and his men descended, Zig-Zag was quick to spot the raid and jumped into a speed boat but was wounded before he sped up the river. The wrapping-up of the gang took no time at all. Zig-Zag had been warned they would shoot if he did not give up; there was nowhere for the wounded animal to go and he was soon apprehended.

The day before, Bruce and the force had raided the Adelaide homes of Kun Hing Won, Zig-Zag and Li Ying Tung as part of the Ping Pong Investigation. They had discovered material at the home of Zig-Zag that would implicate him in the demise of Cornelius Anweir. On the same day, Kun Hing Won had taken a taxi from the airport to his home in Glenelg, a short journey away. He was becoming more concerned that they might be under investigation when he saw police activity outside his house and told the driver to keep going. His worst fears had been realised: he would have to disappear.

"Driver, turn around and head for the marina", he nervously instructed. He paid off the taxi driver by a closed-up shop before they reached the marina. He opened the door to their secure lock-up that MGM used for storage, collected some valuable contraband and stashed it into a kitbag before locking up. With the kitbag on his shoulder, he walked down the jetty to a single mast yacht called *A Piece of Ship*. He threw the kitbag on board and released the mooring ropes before quickly starting the motor and manoeuvring the boat out of the marina. Detective Bruce found details of the ownership of a yacht at the home of Kun Hing Won and went down to the marina, only to see *A Piece of Ship* sailing out to sea. He made a call to the police launch, who chased the yacht, but it was no match for the speedy launch who was forced to ram her when she refused to stop, in full view of an appreciative crowd on the beach, enjoying the drama unfolding before them.

Chapter Eleven

Scotland

It was a wonderful experience, travelling in a sidecar along country roads that wound their way through sumptuous countryside to Westport on a dry but chilly day. They had stopped along the way to view the picturesque Kylemore Abbey. This beautiful setting was another example of Catholic domination – Miles was critical of the wealth of the Church, all extracted from the poor people they conned through the ages. And then there was Croagh Patrick, a mountain for pilgrims to climb that could be seen as they neared Westport. Churches, churches everywhere. Like the temples in Thailand and mosques in Turkey, Iran and Pakistan, they were scattered the length of the country. Who paid for all these churches? he wondered. *The people, of course.*

    He was still coming to terms with Christianity all around; it was the norm, not to be questioned. They were having coffee in Westport when deciding to carry on to Achill Island, to confuse any would-be followers and further explore this beautiful country. It was a B&B and a night in the pub; they knew going north meant they would be watched by everybody and so presented themselves as touring holidaymakers, which they were. The next day it was off to Ballina then the coast road to Sligo, where they stayed in a guest house and enjoyed another night in the pub. Keeping at a leisurely pace they spent the next night in Donegal, still in holiday mode but keeping to themselves. They crossed the border into Ulster through Strabane and never stopped until they arrived at the Giant's Causeway.

After spending a couple of hours exploring this natural wonder of the hexagonal rock pillars, they could not resist the temptation of a further exploration at the Bushmills whiskey distillery. They were disappointed the distillery was closed, and so they decided to have a Bushmills in Bushmills – a loyalist town with an inviting pub that they entered with trepidation, as they felt a concentration of eyes directed upon them. It was not long before the most unsavoury characters came over and encroached around their table in an intimidating manner. The talk was friendly, and after the three tourists had satisfied the locals and established themselves as harmless the hospitality exploded. An offer of a place to stay was graciously accepted, and food and drink was placed on the table, as Trevor saw an opportunity to cover their tail.

A delighted Nee Ding Lu got the lead he had been waiting for when Dirty Mary, with the usual fag hanging from her lip, handed him the *Connaught Tribune*. The heading of "My Balls Itch A Lot" brought an instant smile; he was eager to get going.

"Let's go, Seamus!" he shouted in excitement, but instead he and Seamus Na Maugh left early the next morning for Galway, arriving in Clifden around noon on the Saturday. Seamus had a Chinese mother and was Dirty Mary's nephew, her right-hand man, and the eyes and ears of Dublin's Temple Bar. They all lived above the shop, a good cover for their dodgy activities. Nee Ding Lu was short and wiry, and next to the tall and well-built Seamus they were an unusual-looking sight when they arrived in Clifden. He showed the *Tribune* to Bridget, who was acting as receptionist in the hotel. They were enquiring about My Balls Itch a Lot.

"Oh, you need to see his friend Paddy! He will know where he is. You will find him in Griffins", said Bridget innocently.

"What car does he drive?" Nee Ding Lu asked.

"No car, he was in the sidecar of a motorbike the last I saw him", Bridget replied, and the look of joy on their faces prompted her to think, *What have I done?*

The two men booked in, and Nee Ding Lu phoned Foo Kin Hu from his room. This was breakthrough news; they now knew what to look for. They were on the move, so all ports would be on the alert for a motorbike

A Cork in a Storm

and sidecar. Nee Ding Lu was told to find out which port they were heading to and follow up on any lead he got. It appeared to Foo Kin Hu that there were three of them, possibly four, and the ports would be the best chance of spotting them.

Paddy knew right away who they were. As Nee Ding Lu and Seamus walked into the bar, Paddy began showing Roy the package that Moods had made, and this immediately drew the attention of Nee Ding Lu.

Paddy said, "Roy, I'm on the bus to Galway on Monday. I'll see you when I get back – it could be a few weeks". Paddy left the bar, confident they took the bait and was really getting into the whole drama, happy to do his bit. He smiled to himself when he saw Seamus follow him onto the bus to Galway and smiled again when he followed him onto the bus for Limerick and then another to Cork. The ruse had worked; now Paddy's job was to keep them busy on false trails.

On the night ferry to Swansea, Paddy was still looking over his shoulder at Seamus. *I'll lose him after I pick up the car from Trevor's place.* That was the plan. Paddy's job was to divert the Chinese posse, taking them up blind alleys, and the four would eventually meet up again in Whitby.

After a conversation with Foo Kin Hu, Nee Ding Lu was told to go north as there had been no sighting of the motorbike in Galway. If they went north, they must be heading for Larne. *I'll see if I can pick up a trail before that,* thought Nee Ding Lu, as he was now on his own and still bathing in glory after the breakthrough find. He was asking questions in all the towns going north, but he had not picked up any leads until he enquired about the motorbike in Bushmills.

Trevor leaned over to Tony, the most frightening looking member of their new found friends and explained more details of their trip and that there were some Chinese looking for them. It was not long before laughter engulfed the party, and laughter had been in short supply for a long time in this town.

"Here we are in the middle of a conflict with no end, and you guys bring us another one", said Tony, "but do not worry, we will look after you". They had not had such a fun night in town for a long time, as they had the clientele enthralled with tales of the Far East, so different to what life was like for them. Miles sang an Australian bush ballad that nobody had heard before and the pints kept coming over.

How looks could be deceiving, thought Miles, as Tony, turned out to be the most gracious host, reminding Miles of the kindness shown by strangers to himself on his extraordinary journey. Finding that human kindness here in this troubled arena was quite humbling and hope for peace would come by this understanding of others without the prejudice.

After a hearty breakfast, Miles left Tony his address, saying, "Thanks very much, Tony, stay cool, keep in touch and ciao", as they rode off to Larne. The two-hour ferry crossing would get them to Stranraer in Scotland around seven in the evening.

They had all noticed the eyes upon them as they disembarked at the terminal and took the road to Glasgow. "We have a tail", shouted Trevor, after being unable to shake off the black Mercedes that had followed them into Ayr and was still there when they reached Kilmarnock. "We will have to lose them!" he yelled. "Hold tight."

They managed to evade their pursuers in Glasgow for a short enough time to have a coffee and a pow-wow.

"How did they know what to look for? Who told them"? said Miles.

"It does not matter now…we are in transport that is easily spotted. Where do we go?" voiced Moods, eager to stay positive and keep moving.

Miles said, "We must lose them in Edinburgh, and lose them before we take the road to North Berwick. After we are sure we have lost them, we can call on a friend of mine there who can hide us for a while".

Trevor said, "So be it; we will dodge our way through the night. I hope your friend is hospitable. It could be late".

Once they took off, they were soon spotted again and were followed into Edinburgh but were confident they had lost their markers as they took the road to North Berwick and then pulled up at three o'clock in the morning in the drive of Cardboard Colin. Colin had got his name in Kathmandu as he always ended up with the roach, the last bit of the joint. He had no immediate neighbours to be disturbed by the knock on the bungalow door. It took a few minutes after a concerned Colin opened the door for his bleary eyes to become sparkling with the surprise on his doorstep, and then fill with joy as he embraced Miles.

"Come in! Tell me all about it", a fully awake and inquisitive Colin said excitedly.

"First, Col, we must hide the bike. Can you help?" Miles said urgently.

Colin responded, "Sure, we can do a swap with my car in the garage. I will get the keys".

In no time the bike and sidecar were behind closed doors and Miles introduced his friends, saying they were all tired and could they explain in the morning. "Why, of course. Make yourself at home – there are two beds and a couch. I'll leave you to sort yourselves out and I look forward to breakfast", the intrigued Colin replied.

The smell of bacon frying in the pan, bread toasting and the kettle boiling had them up mid-morning. Colin had been an excited listener when he exclaimed, "Fantastic, absolutely fascinating", after Miles, Moods and Trevor had collectively told the story so far.

"We need to stay low for a while yet", said Miles. "These Chinamen are very persistent."

Colin queried, "You never mentioned the package in Nepal".

"No, I was told to forget it was there, and I did. It is still here", said Miles, patting his bag made in Penang; it has not moved.

Trevor, who now appeared to be taking control, came in with, "We need to dismantle the sidecar, Colin, and when the time is right, I will take off on the bike. It would be great if you could help the boys on their way".

Miles was enthusiastic when he explained his plan. "They will not expect me to go home again, and I had told Paddy to meet us at my folks' place in Whitby. It is not far down the road. I can see Ma and Pa as they must be worried, so we must go there."

Colin was adamant when he said, "For the time being, there is no reason to go anywhere". He placed a biscuit tin on the table. "You have not forgotten, have you, Itch?' A smiling Colin opened the tin to reveal a bag of grass and all the makings.

It was Friday, 12th of April, just two weeks to D-Day. They had had a wonderful time at Colin's, who would go out daily for groceries and beer. Even Jan turned up to see Miles, and got involved with the drinking, smoking, and playing cards. There was not a care in the world, in their safe hideout.

"We are back on track now", said Trevor. "We should move out tomorrow. This has been fantastic, but we have imposed on Colin for far too long. I will go to London and I will ring you at your place, Itchy, in a few days for an update."

"This has been an absolute pleasure, and I shall be waiting with anticipation to hear the outcome", the accommodating Colin was happy to reply.

Paddy had slept with one eye open, and he could feel the presence of Seamus close by as he climbed off the ferry and walked over to the taxi rank. "Here, driver. Take me to this address in Cockett", said Paddy, as he got in quickly, conscious of the movements of Seamus. He paid for the taxi outside the house with the Buddha in the garden and began to walk up the drive. Seamus arrived in a following taxi and the gubbons came speeding up after watching the arrivals.

"What do you want?" said a cornered Paddy.

"The package in your bag", said Seamus. "Give it to me."

Paddy frowned when he said, "It looks like I have no choice", as the three men came in closer. He fumbled as he took the package out of his bag.

"I will take that", said the Hat, snatching at the package. "We leave right away", he exclaimed, as all three men got into the pale blue Viva and drove away at speed.

Paddy was enjoying himself, giggling like a naughty boy as he uncovered the car and drove into Swansea for breakfast.

Li Ying Tung was sitting at the desk talking with Foo Kin Hu in the office of MGM when the gubbons swaggered through the door and placed the package in front of them. They both smiled, knowing the gubbons had fallen for the package deception before, and so it was again, after the package revealed a book called *The Search for the Holy Grail*. The Hat was distraught and began shouting something in Chinese as a much-heated discussion followed, but Foo Kin Hu controlled the show; he ordered the gubbons back to find the car and the red-bearded man called Paddy. He could be the one to lead them to their elusive adversaries. No avenue would be left unchecked. Seamus had impressed Foo Kin Hu and was told to keep up the surveillance in Whitby.

As Seamus was going out the door, he turned and asked, "Why, Whitby? Is there a chance we could find them there?"

Li Ying Tung replied, "Foo Kin Hu knows".

Meanwhile, Paddy had the keys to the house and had stopped for provisions before driving back and letting himself in, where he would wait to be found. He left the car on the drive like a homing beacon and settled down on the sofa, happy and content with the plan so far. To his amusement, the pale blue Viva arrived and parked across the street the next day, as he was placing incense by the Buddha. He continued this ritual every day and would even wave at the gubbons, who would grimace with embarrassment. After a week of torment for the gubbons, Paddy decided to take them touring and drove to Bath, to visit his cousin, Tommy the Dancer, a name he got after being saved from accidently hanging himself. They both had a great time catching up on the news from Clifden and drinking the local cider, while all the time, the gubbons sat and observed from a distance and then had to sleep in the car on a cold winter's night.

Paddy and Tommy had a day out at Stonehenge towing their tail around the countryside and irritating the gubbons even more, finishing off the day drinking Marsden's and Worthington E beers in a last remaining bar for men only, leaving the gubbons to spend another cold and miserable night in the car, and it only got worse for the tormented pair the next day.

Paddy had spent a couple of enjoyable days with Cousin Tommy and was going to miss the gubbons' attention when he easily lost them on his way to Aunt Gronya in Birmingham, leaving the gubbons bamboozled and in despair once again. He left the car outside the house, covered with the tarpaulin he had brought with him, promising it would not be there long. The next day being Saturday, he took an early train to Newcastle and then a bus into Whitby; he was attracted to the site of the abbey and the daunting one hundred and ninety-nine steps and could not resist the climb. The abbey was worth the visit, the inspiration for Bram Stoker's novel *Dracula*. There was a church and a graveyard with many weathered gravestones. *That is a long way to haul a coffin*, he thought, as he surveyed the town from this bleak hilltop, before descending to knock on the door of Pa Zytchalot.

Miles and Moods had been dropped off earlier and had watched Paddy approach. The door opened, and Paddy was quickly ushered inside. Ma and Pa had been full of questions and Paddy's arrival had them even more intrigued. Over the next few days Ma and Pa learnt all about the ongoing adventure and were happy to help them in their quest, by having somewhere for them to hide. Pa came in one morning saying, "A picture postcard of Bushmills Distillery has arrived for Itch. Is that you, Mibald? Here it is".

Miles laughed as he read out loud to Moods. "Chinaman on slow boat to China. From Tony. Trevor will love this."

Miles's ma was known as Ma to everyone, with her name being Marjorie, and she was enjoying looking after the boys amid all the drama. With the days ticking over nicely, it would all be over soon, until Paddy popped out for cigarettes and came back distressed. "I think I was spotted by that tail from Ireland. If so, there will be a herd of them up here before too long."

"He is right. It's time to move, like now. We will take the bus into Newcastle and see if anyone follows, then go on from there. This is the last leg, let's not screw it up", a controlled Miles said.

This was met with an equally determined response from Moods, who declared, "Let's go".

Seamus had spotted him alright, and phoned Fu Kin Hu for instructions. The Hat and his number two had entered the office of MGM. The Hat was once again upset about having to report a failure; he was quiet as he listened to Foo Kin Hu tell Li Ying Tung that they crossed on the ferry from Larne into Scotland but lost the trail in Edinburgh. They could not stay hidden for long. Li Ying Tung had been concerned about the disappearance of Nee Ding Lu, who had followed them up north and was never seen or heard of again.

The Hat was about to speak when the phone rang. It was Seamus. Smiles broke out with the news of the sighting, as Seamus was told to stick like glue, keep in touch and report all movements. He was sending the dynamic duo up to help. The Hat smiled with relief at not having to embarrass himself again, saying, "We are on our way".

As they turned to go, Foo Kin Hu cried, "Where are you going? I have not told you yet – we will wait till we hear from Seamus".

Ma and Pa wished them luck, with Pa saying, "Believe in the power of prayer", which made Miles remember where he was, so he just smiled and said nothing, as the three troupers set out on the final leg. Trevor had rung in, and they planned to rendezvous on Wednesday the 24th, at an address in St Albans, a town steeped in history, and a convenient location coming up to D-Day.

A Cork in a Storm

Paddy said, "There's yeh man", to Miles and Moods, as Seamus Na Maugh was leaning up against the wall keeping a close watch on them. They were twice as alert when he followed them onto the bus.

"We could go to Birmingham and pick up the car. We may as well now and have some control over our movements", said Miles.

"Show us the way, Paddy."

Seamus was still in close attendance as they got off the train in Birmingham but was soon chasing shadows, as these boys were now very good at disappearing. Aunt Gronya was accommodating, and they would camp down on the lounge floor, safe for another night at least, while a bemused Seamus would once again ring in with the news that he had lost them in Birmingham.

"Do not worry, we know their movements. They will be heading back here. I will send the Dynamic Duo to pick you up. Come back to London." Li Ying Tung was worried. Only days remained before the second reading of the will and disaster if they could not destroy the package.

Miles was thinking about the car — what a car it had turned out to be! Each of them had their own adventure and now together they would travel to St Albans. They had not been followed and rang the bell of the house lived in by John Johnson, a friend of Trevor Trevor who was expecting them and helped them to quickly throw the tarp over the car on the drive and shuffled them into the semi-detached hideaway.

Johnno, as he introduced himself was an Australian Vietnam vet and well acquainted with their quest, after being recruited by Trevor. Miles was delighted when he said he was marching on Anzac Day and asked if he could join in. Johnno was equally delighted to find a fellow vet and said, "You Uc Dai Loi" with Miles replying, "You cheap Charlie," then both breaking into song, "Uc Dai Loi, Cheap Charlie, he no buy me Saigon tea, Saigon tea cost many, any P, Uc Dai Loi he cheap Charlie", then dived into a question-and-answer conversation. Johnno had served in the same battalion in Vietnam, only three years earlier than Miles, in 1966. They had lots in common, becoming instant friends, and the party began when Trevor turned up. The beer came out of the fridge as he excitedly told them they would all be staying at the Strand Palace Hotel after the Anzac Day parade and outlined details for Friday. It was an early morning start to make the eleven o'clock parade and Miles told Johnno he did not have his medals.

"No worries, mate, I can fix that", he said as he brought out a Polaroid camera. He took a picture of his own medals and pinned it on Miles's chest, to everybody's amusement.

They got to the cenotaph in time for the march and Miles handed his bag to Moods. An ex-RSM who was conducting the parade came over to Miles, clearly not amused with the photo, and told Miles he could not march, but he was soon persuaded by the support from other vets, and realising this was pure Aussie improvisation, told him to fall in. Miles felt so proud, so Australian, as he marched to the pipes and drums of the military band. He had become a man of peace and yet would give respect to everybody who put on a uniform and obeyed the call.

Once a soldier, always a soldier; it was the mateship you never lost. Experience was the way to understanding; he had not realised his experience had affected him in such a profound way. He knew the pride his fellow veterans were feeling and the sorrow remembering fallen comrades. The poignant sound of the bugle playing the "Last Post" never failed to bring a tear. The marchers then attended a service at Westminster Abbey.

As Miles entered, he was struck by the magnificence of the abbey; he was stunned by the sheer splendour of the occasion, as trumpets sounded and the choir was singing. Officials in historic attire added to the pomp and ceremony that had Miles mesmerised. *This splendid display of respect could only happen here,* thought Miles, *in England with all its regal history.*

Loostea and Val were waiting with the others in the Red Lion on Whitehall; they had all viewed the parade and gave a warm reception to Johnno and Miles when the parade finished, the end of the march signalling a scramble to the bar, as the pub was soon heaving on this special day. Miles and Johnno had been talking with all the old diggers, hearing stories from WWII and Korean veterans. Vietnam vets were the juniors and would respectfully listen and enjoy the company.

The beers and tears flowed before the farewells; the event had given temporary respite to the job in hand until they left the inn and disaster struck. They had protected the Holy Grail through many adventures and thousands of miles, only to have the bag snatched on the eve of completion.

The devastated group were sombre as they taxied to the Strand Palace Hotel for the last supper.

It was Wednesday, and there were grim faces in the office of MGM as Li Ying Tung spelt out the situation: "We do not know where they are, but we do know where they are going. We know the two cousins will be going, too, so put a double surveillance on them right away – they will lead us to the package". Foo Kin Hu knew what to do after the Dynamic Duo had followed Loostea and Val to Covent Garden and lost them in the usual fashion. The double surveillance worked, as Seamus rang in from Whitehall, reporting that they were at the Anzac Day parade.

"Stay there, I am coming over", said Foo Kin Hu. "I be there very quick, maybe in ten minutes."

Seamus had spotted Paddy, then he had seen Miles hand over the bag to Moods and told Foo Kin Hu when he arrived.

"The bag, that is the bag we want, you must go and get it. We will wait till the time is right, I will create diversion, and you grab the bag. This is our chance for big reward!" The opportunity arose as Itchy followed the others out of the Red Lion Inn. All were merry when they saw Foo Kin Hu in his black pyjamas walk towards them. Miles and Johnno turned pale at the sight of this Viet Cong lookalike and froze long enough for Seamus to snatch the bag and get away before the drunken party could respond.

Chapter Twelve

London

They had chosen the Strand Palace Hotel, as it was only a short walking distance to the solicitor's office of Bone & Idle, as the group entered like lambs to the slaughter for the three o'clock deadline reading of the will. The office was of good size with large windows, but it still felt stuffy, with files strewn across the floor in what seemed like heaps of disorder. There were a dozen chairs in front of the large desk in similar disorder, with the Chinese representation occupying prominent positions.

A smiling Li Ying Tung and Foo Kin Hu had been horrified to find the bag did not contain the right package, only a book called *From Here to Eternity*. This was the third time they had been fooled and it was now the moment of truth. They acknowledged the group as they took their places; they were clearly expecting the worst and unable to look at them. The meeting started with, "I am Mr Idle of Bone & Idle, and we are here for the reading of the second part of the will of Cornelius Anweir. First, may I have the package as part of the terms outlined in the will".

"Well," began Loostea, before Milcs interrupted, taking the package from inside his shirt and handing it to her, saying, "I took it out of its pocket for the first time the night before we went on the march and replaced it with a book from Johnno's bookcase, feeling it would be safer on my person, being so close to the finish. Forgive me for being quiet, but with only me knowing, I thought that was the safe way to go, as well".

The majority mood in the office instantly changed from one of gloom to one of relief, as a smiling Loostea kissed Miles and handed the package to Mr Idle.

He was examining the package while referring to his notes, and he was about to continue when Trevor spoke up. "Before you open that, sir, I have something to say."

What now? thought Miles, turning his head to Moods, who whispered, "It gets more intriguing by the minute".

"I have not been completely truthful to you all by not declaring that I was once a detective for the Adelaide police force, as was Johnno. Only Val and Loostea knew I was also operating under cover for the Adelaide police. I was on a case involving Ping Pong Industries when I met Val, who had been asking questions about his grandfather. Your grandfather had given a contract document to his personal solicitor, Mr Frank Leigh, to read. After a thorough scanning, he informed Cornelius and alerted us of the danger he could be in, if Cornelius could not make the date as stated, which is today. Ping Pong Industries would take control of his holding, an inclusion that had not been mentioned. It was then, Mr Leigh told us, that they devised a plan, that in the event of his demise, the package would expose the truth, with the evidence that Cornelius would gather. We had strong information that it would expose their operation but without enough proof, there could be no prosecution. I was leaving the force to come back home to look after Mum and Dad's house while they went to live on a canal boat for a year or two, and I told Loostea and Val I would help. I was intrigued, and I believed Ping Pong had a major involvement in the demise of Cornelius Anweir. I was given permission to continue the investigation under a special licence, sort of freelance but still attached to South Australian police. Loostea and I would meet again in Chiang Mai for an update on the package and where I purchased a beautiful Buddha. I was to get here today to witness this moment of truth."

There were gasps and murmurings. Foo Kin Hu and a fidgeting Li Ying Tung looked at Mr Idle as he said, "Is there anybody else wishing to speak before I disclose the contents of the package? No, then I shall proceed. First, I shall read the summary of my counterpart in Adelaide, Mr Frank Leigh."

He began, "When Cornelius Anweir was alerted to the consequences of such a contract, he became concerned and began to fill in his diary in my office, where it would be kept safe. He had suspected wrongdoings by his partners and now he was collecting evidence that Zig-Zag could make people disappear who were not in his act and feared for his own safety. We insisted the contract include a clause, that in the event of him being unable to attend the offices of Bone & Idle in London at the time and date specified, a blood relative would attend to honour the contract. Cornelius and I had become friends, with him coming into the office daily, and when he died of natural causes, I would still ensure his wishes would be carried out. I have read all the entries in his diary, which does hold incriminating evidence against his partners, namely Ping Pong Industries".

The face of Li Ying Tung had been contorting with every disclosure and at this point, she lunged forward and snatched the package then threw it to Foo Kin Hu, who had already moved to the door and was out before he could be tackled but with Moods in hot pursuit. Johnno had Li Ying Tung in an arm lock, as they rang the police, before eventually, Mr Idle called for calm amid the commotion. After a while when things had calmed down, he said, "If I may carry on, I am sure the story will unfold".

He cleared his throat and was about to continue when the police arrived, along with Moods and Foo Kin Hu. The police were soon satisfied with what had happened and they arrested Li Ying Tung and Foo Kin Hu, taking them away amid their loud protests.

"Now, may I continue?" Mr Idle humoured, with the package now back on the table. "Cornelius gave me instructions, that in the event of his demise, I was to show the diary to the police before preparing the package to be presented at the reading of the will. The police kept the diary, as the evidence was too important, and proposed I prepare something else. Cornelius had intended to show this book to the police but died before saying why it could be of interest. It looked insignificant to me and so I prepared this book instead of the diary. I trust this will not have inconvenienced anyone, as it may still prove important."

"*Inconvenience anyone*, that could turn out to be a massive understatement", said Miles.

"My signature on the book will further authenticate the package to fulfil the terms of the contract". Mr Idle began to unwrap the parcel. It was strange for Miles to watch it being undressed after all the adventures they had been through.

This is it, the moment of truth.

First out of the maroon velvet bag was the document, to comply with the terms, but then the eagerly waiting ensemble groaned as a copy *Conjuring Tricks for Beginners* by Zig-Zag was revealed, with the signature of Frank Leigh across the cover.

"What?" cried Miles. "What does this mean?"

Trevor would once again take the floor. "I was in contact with Detective Bruce of the Adelaide police yesterday for a long time and I can now tell you that they have Zig-Zag and Kun Hing Won in custody for the murder of Cornelius Anweir. I could not disclose this to you earlier with Li Ying Tung being present, as she is also implicated. May I have the book please, Mr Idle?"

Everybody looked at each other wondering what was coming next as Trevor opened the book. He flicked through the pages, looking for a clue, and found it inside the back cover with the words "Wipe Me", which had been handwritten. Trevor asked for a damp cloth as everybody became more intrigued. He gently wiped the inside of the back cover and letters began to appear. After he had inspected it for a short while, a smiling Trevor held the book aloft declaring, "This is it. In here are names and bank details of many accounts used in their operation; this is what is going to nail them. Your grandfather has been a hero. This will expose them totally and will lead to the whole crime syndicate collapsing. It will be an enormous help to the force with ongoing investigations around the country. This book is even more important than before and is vital evidence that will connect them to the Triads in Sydney and Melbourne. Horse race fixing was among the illegal activities, while money laundering for the Triads was their main role with Li Ying Tung controlling that operation, using MGM as a front. Your grandfather was not fooled by his partners and knew they were crooks; he delved deeply into the accounts to discover what they were doing and how they worked, which probably cost him his life".

Loostea had been listening with intent interest when she asked, 'You said 'murder'. Why do you say that when the death certificate states he died of a heart attack?"

"True, however the cause of the cardiac arrest was due to the regular ingestion of a toxic herb that had been mixed in with his pipe tobacco, quantities of which have been found in Zig-Zag's possession. Lab analysis confirmed that the tobacco mixture would trigger a cardiac arrest."

Loostea was nodding her head and beckoning Trevor to continue, eager for more.

"An entry in your grandfather's diary showed that he had received a gift of pipe tobacco from Zig-Zag in the casino. That was one week before he died."

He raised the book again, emphasizing its importance. "I have not told you that this book is also used to send coded messages to the gangs in Sydney and Melbourne, and this secret message written by your grandfather contains all the details of how, when, and where their business is done and how to decipher the code".

Valentine had been open-mouthed during the revelations and asked, "So, what this tells me is – and please tell me if I am wrong – had Frank Leigh given this book to the police, as Granddad would have done, and prepared something else instead, none of this would have happened".

There were gasps, as the realization sank in. They were wide-eyed and open-mouthed as they all looked at each other. Of course, Mr Frank Leigh's statement of insignificance was majestically wrong, and Miles began to grin before they all erupted in a despairing bout of laughter.

"What happens now?" asked Val.

Trevor was apologetic as he replied, "All assets of Ping Pong Industries have been impounded and nothing can be released until the investigation is complete. That could take some time. Your grandfather has been instrumental in bringing down their crooked operation, which will help when calculating the final value of his estate, which will then go to your parents."

A confused Miles said in a crestfallen voice, "Is that it then? The adventure is over, we did it all for nothing and didn't have to?"

"We had a great time, though", said Moods.

"Would not have missed it", said Paddy.

"In the final reckoning by the state", said Trevor, "there will be a reward and award which will involve all of us".

Loostea smiled as she invited everybody to dinner, but not before Mr Idle prompted them to remain until the reading was complete.

"We are sorry, Mr Idle, of course. But may I point out the book is now vital and important evidence", said Trevor.

"Looks like it is not over yet, guys", said Moods before Mr Idle replied to Trevor, "Thank you, I am aware of its importance as Mr Leigh concludes in his summary, and I suggest the book stays here in the office safe until collected by the police on Monday when I reopen the office".

There was a pause as they all looked at each other and Miles said, "I suppose we will have to. It just seems so anticlimactic, like we did it, but we didn't".

They all agreed and watched Mr Idle place the book in its maroon velvet cover and secure it in the safe. They made their way out onto the Strand and saw a Chinese restaurant not far away. "That looks appropriate", said Loostea, and as they moved off, Miles thought he caught a glimpse of the Hat.

They entered the restaurant and were shown to the round banquet table that would seat all seven of them. "Here we are, the Seven Musketeers, said Paddy.

"There were only three, Paddy; you are getting mixed up", said Johnno, laughing with all the others.

"Well, there are seven now", came the reply.

While the mood was light, Miles spoke up. "I think we should keep an eye on the office over the weekend with those gubbons still on the loose."

"If we arrive there when they open on Monday, it should be alright. The gubbons have no boss now, but they may still hold a grudge", said Trevor.

"Aye, that makes sense. You know, I feel like I did when I returned from Vietnam. I'd done it, but it felt empty…what was it for? And yet I was proud to be part of that adventure. I had done my duty, made incredible friendships, like now – it is the experience that bonds you together, we have survived an incredible journey. Not many can boast of an adventure like ours. You are right, Paddy, we are the Seven Musketeers."

They were all smiling now as they tucked into the banquet with enthusiasm. "You must learn to use the chopsticks, Itchy. Shovelling in rice with your fingers does not blend in well with Western etiquette", Loostea said, smiling.

"Oh, I am sorry, force of habit", returned Miles.

She carried on, hoping to receive the answers she wanted to hear. "Well, Itchy, what will you do now?"

He smiled and said, "I think I would like to go back to Ireland. I made a promise I must keep, and I want to find out who rumbled us. It has been bothering me. So, if you don't mind, Paddy, I'll go back with you. I will need to go home first to put Ma and Pa's minds at ease, see cardboard Col and then drive to Liverpool to drop off Moods".

"What for?" cried Moods. "If you crossed back into Ireland from Stranraer and me with you, we could go see Tony. He would love the story, and I would also like to know how he put the Chinaman on a slow boat back to China".

"There you go, Paddy, the Three Irish Musketeers", laughed Johnno.

Through all the merriment a confused Loostea could not hide her disappointment when she asked, "I thought you and I were going back to Australia, Itchy. Val and I are going back to see what the outcome is, and I am staying. You know, the warm weather, the space, a land where opportunities abound… You are a war veteran, you must feel a connection. Why go to Ireland? It is cold, wet, and full of Catholics".

She had laid it on thick, but she had spoken with emotion in her voice, almost pleading with him to reconsider; she did not want to lose her man.

"It is always my intention to return to Australia, I belong there. I am Australian, it is in my very being, but I have other roads to travel first. Ireland is beautiful – the people, the music, the scenery. Okay, it can get cold and wet, but I have learnt a lot over these past years. When I went to Australia, I wanted to be Australian, I wanted to be one of the people. I suppose being called up for National Service helped me achieve that. It is being committed to where you live and I loved Ireland, Connemara especially, enough to make me want to return. No matter where you are in the world, you accept their culture and respect their beliefs. Who knows? I may become a Tri-National. Now that could be confusing."

"Anyway", cried Trevor, "we will all keep in touch".

Val shouted, "All for one!"

"And one for all!" came a unanimous and loud response. They were as one, each proud to be a Musketeer.

"I will stay with you two, if I may", said Trevor, "and TIM can go back with Johnno. We can all meet up again at the office first thing Monday morning".

"TIM?" questioned Paddy.

"Yeah, The Irish Musketeers", he answered to more laughter on a night of mixed feelings.

A smiling Miles was thinking, *We will never meet like this again. Tomorrow, it is a memory. I wish I had a camera.*

They finished their feast with a toast to Granddad, Cornelius Anweir, the true hero, and ambled out onto the Strand. To their horror, as they approached the office of Bone & Idle, they could see a lot of police activity and hurried to the scene. They found that Mr Idle had been held up and robbed; he had been forced to open the safe and the book was gone. "It is not over yet, comrades", said a dejected Miles.

The gubbons had watched the comings and goings of the afternoon meeting, from a building where they could see the entrance and the large office window. The empty office space that was To Let, opposite Bone & Idle, provided the gubbons with an ideal vantage point. They had been shown in by the unsuspecting caretaker, who was bound and gagged as they observed the meeting from their excellent viewing position. When the Musketeers left the Bone & Idle office, the gubbons pounced and forced Mr Idle, who was locking up, back into the office at gunpoint, where he offered little resistance and opened the safe as he was staring into the barrel of a gun. They left Mr Idle tied up and took off with the book, as the Hat looked in wonder at the maroon velvet package that he had travelled many miles to find. He sang "We did it, Number Two, we did it. We had to get tough, but we did it. I am so happy! The Master will be pleased."

"Where would they go? It must be the gubbons," said Moods.

"Well, obviously, they do not know their boss is locked up", said Trevor. "Now, from my time watching the watchers, I found out the boss operated out of the office of MGM in Soho, and I reckon that is where they will head. We better tell the police what we know."

It was late when they left the station, but a plan had been put in place. Loostea said she would continue to carry the tab and that they should all book in the hotel again, ready for more drama in the morning.

It was Saturday morning in Soho. The office of MGM was occupied by a Chinese undercover detective, who did not have long to wait before the phone rang. Nearby Chinatown was covered with plainclothes police, while the Musketeers were deployed in Covent Garden, not too far away but enough not to alert the gubbons.

"Hello, MGM office, Yu Wang." The phone went dead, and a well-informed Yu Wang would sit and wait, but not for long.

The gubbons were having breakfast in the Charring Cross Hotel when the Hat said, "We see Li Ying Tung and Foo Kin Hu taken away, we must be careful, Number Two. I ring up first". The Hat made his call then put the phone down.

"Who Yu Wang, Number Two?" he asked, as Number Two just shrugged his shoulders without speaking.

"I ring again…Hello, who Yu Wang?" He covered the mouthpiece with his hand and said, "He say Kun Hing Won sent him to collect parcel, Number Two, and do we have it".

There was a long pause as the gubbons exchanged anxious glances before the Hat replied, "I have parcel. Where we meet? I think office being watched, maybe". He was nodding his head saying, "Okay, okay", as he listened to Yu Wang. "Covent Garden Market, I got it, you wear white suit, I find you. We see you one hour."

Trevor had phoned in to the MGM office from a public phone in the market when they arrived, and Yu Wang took the number and told him to stay close. Trevor lifted the phone when it rang later to hear him say, "They are coming your way, so are we. Make yourself scarce." The Musketeers had scattered themselves around the busy market after the alert, each keeping low.

Yu Wang strolled through the market in his distinctive white suit carrying Miles's travel bag and sat down in the cafe area, as if glowing in the dark. Through the crowds emerged the Hat, heading towards Yu Wang. When Miles walked out in front of him, the Hat screamed, "It is a trap, Number Two, run!" Each way they went, a Musketeer would block their path, gradually encompassing them until there was nowhere to go.

Yu Wang was there to disarm them of a cigarette lighter that was a fake gun and retrieve the parcel; everybody's relief was accompanied with pity when they saw the Hat crying as he was led away.

"I reckon we can all go home now", said Moods. They all looked at each other; they knew the adventure was over, but a new one had already started as every day was an adventure. Miles was happy to be reunited with his bag full of memories as they strolled out of the market and out onto the road, when he stopped, once again fascinated by a colour TV in a window.

"Did you know", he said, "fifty years ago they would go to a cinema to watch silent movies? Now they have colour television in their homes. What is it going to be like in another fifty years? You may be able to carry a TV in your pocket".

It was now mid-afternoon, and all their plans had changed. Everything had all now been resolved, and they would never be the same again. "We cannot leave like this; let us all stay one more night and have a victory dinner and tell stories", said Loostea. This was greeted with a loud and unanimous chorus of, "Yeah, yeah, yeah", as they quickened their step, all beaming with satisfaction at the success of their mission. They were all in good humour as they sat down to dinner, with each having a funny story to tell about the Hat.

The conversation drifted between culture and religion as they finished their meal, prompting Johnno to speak. "Now, TIM, what did you learn on your spiritual journey? I am the only one of us here who has not been touched by Buddhism or anything else other than Christianity, and you three have experienced a great deal. I have always been a Christian, never had a reason to question it. Enlighten me, I am curious."

"Understanding", said Paddy, "or trying to understand human nature and why people act the way they do. To stop complaining, knowing that life is not fair and that you are not important. Self-awareness, knowing your faults and accepting them while all the time you keep trying to rectify them, and then by developing good habits of positive thinking, you will be ready when difficult times come your way. I am now happy not having a belief, or having a belief in non-believing, allowing an open mind to expand in the search for truth, but it is important that we have a laugh along the way. I was born and bred in Ireland, a good God-fearing Catholic until I went on my journey with an open mind, in search of the truth. In Buddhism, I found a way to be happy and that happiness is a choice. If anything, I believe in the truth, and the greatest truth of all is 'I know nothing'. We have a duty to be happy; not everybody wants to experience adventure in life, which is fine. They are the lucky ones, content with their lot, like those with faith who do not question their belief. I can live with all of them, and I will enjoy every moment of every day, happy just keeping it simple and focusing on the moment, with the belief that I can survive by just being me. Now, isn't that the truth?"

Moods was buzzing, having an opportunity to talk about his journey when he said, "Thank you, everybody, I have never felt so spiritually beautified. I have had the adventure of a lifetime. If I had not questioned Christianity and embraced Buddhism, it would never have happened for me… Buddhism, a religion of no religion, teaching self-awareness and that happiness comes from within. The meeting we had in Bangkok at the temple of the Emerald Buddha convinced me to listen to my thoughts. I was taught to allow them to drift by like clouds, not to cling onto them, all the time knowing things never stay the same. Letting go is an important part of Buddhist guidance: Free yourself from attachments to relieve suffering. Do not clutter the mind with things out of your control, let go. I had become aware we are, what we think.

"Ugli Twat was a good teacher when he spoke of the influences we endure every day, like the need for money, the people conditioning newspapers, persistent advertising and noise. I find solitude and meditation rewarding, connecting with the flow of the universe, not resisting it. I am now my own man believing in my inner self, accepting my own limitations to find that inner peace. The making of money is no longer a controlling influence in my life; not making excuses and accepting the truth no matter how hard it is, has become more important. Just being content with what I have, living every moment, sharing knowledge and being able to accept new knowledge with equal clarity. So, this adventure we have enjoyed was not about reward, it just seemed right, spiritual, and I have loved it."

"I was at that meeting in the temple with my head in turmoil, as you can imagine", said Loostea, "but I left feeling comfortable in myself. I had a confidence in my inner self that I would instinctively know what to do, no matter what may come my way. Now, Itchy, I am looking forward to your tale".

Everyone turned to Itchy with equal enthusiasm, and Johnno was beaming with delight that his question had revealed so much. He was taking it all in and digesting every word.

Miles was in deep thought as silence fell and he began to tell his tale.

"I actually rekindled my spiritual journey in beautiful Bali, an island paradise that I found hard to leave. I had already abandoned religion and let go of God and all that holy shit; I was on a clean sheet, if you like, I had a passion for knowledge, and Bali was so unique, so different it gave me a hunger to find out more about other cultures and the effect on the people. My whole journey was spiritual, learning about other religions, feeling them, living them. I absorbed so much of Hindu wisdom in India, but it was in Kathmandu at a meeting with the PWC that I began to think logically about religion. We were chasing the truth about religion and God and concluding that belonging to a belief would corrupt your thoughts and you would not have a free and open mind.

"The PWC was the unofficial People's World Council, only one of its kind, and we had a lot of fun searching for truth. Many thought-provoking questions would be asked, and it was at one of these sessions that ancient history was explored. This was a subject I knew little about but became awakened and enthralled about these structures that were built many thousands of years ago, using massive stones weighing many tons. That really interested me. Highly intelligent civilisations completely disappeared that had immense knowledge which disappeared with them. Astronomy was a clear influence in their culture; the engineering involved to build the temples was so technically advanced that a lot of people believe they were not built by humans, but rather by aliens – a theory that needs to be explored more thoroughly. There are many unexplained mysteries in this world that nothing can be dismissed. What I realised was the enormity of mankind: we are mere passengers in time, guests on this planet in a wondrous and infinite universe. The main truth that we all agreed on was that we know nothing; there is always something more to know.

"So, with that knowledge, nothing was established at our council, but we concluded that we all have a part to play in evolution and not to rush it, just enjoy it and go with the flow. A wise old guru in Benares told me the world is out of balance and that evolution is slow; it may take a thousand years or two or more before balance is achieved. We must hope that one day it will be. Our time is now. Life is not yesterday, not tomorrow, but now, today. The world is in a constant state of change. What we do today has a consequence tomorrow – we must teach the children well. Everybody is unique, we all take different paths in life, and everybody has a part to play in progressing the world into a better place. Today, now, life is what you make it. That is life, that is God.

"Then again, I could be wrong."
"I love you, Itchy", cried Loostea.